D0240003

'I MIND
THE TIME'

'I MIND THE TIME'

Country tales of village life

Roger Anthony Freeman

BLANDFORD PRESS

LONDON . NEW YORK . SYDNEY

First published in the UK 1988 by Blandford Press,
Artillery House, Artillery Row, London, SW1P 1RT

Copyright © 1988 Roger Anthony Freeman

Distributed in the United States by
Sterling Publishing Co, Inc,
2 Park Avenue, New York, NY 10016

Distributed in Australia by
Capricorn Link (Australia) Pty Ltd
PO Box 665, Lane Cove, NSW 2066

British Library Cataloguing in Publication Data

Freeman, Roger A.
 I mind the time : country goings on.
 I. Title
 823'.914[F]   PR6056.R42/

ISBN 0 7137 2010 7

Typeset by Inforum Ltd, Portsmouth
Printed and bound in Great Britain
by Mackays of Chatham Ltd.

Contents

Preface

When I was a boy my father employed a magnificent countryman named Horace Ellis. He was hard-working and skilled; proud but possessed of a delightful sense of humour. His life spanned near to a century; as a child he saw the railways come and when he died man was reaching for the moon. In his dotage Horrie liked nothing better than to recall the past, the people and rural happenings. Sit him down with a glass of ale or cup of tea and he would begin. Always with the opening line: 'I mind the time when . . .'

Now it is my turn to Mind The Time, although from nowhere near such advanced years. Nevertheless, in the following pages I recall some of the characters and goings-on from long and not so long ago. And, as is the right of any country storyteller, I have perhaps coloured them a little in the telling.

Roger Anthony Freeman

The Scene Hereabouts
An Introduction

East Anglia can be viewed on a map either as Britain's hefty posterior or as its advanced pregnancy, depending on whether this isle is imagined as facing Ireland or continental Europe. The area is well represented in our early history, boasting Britain's oldest recorded town and attracting considerable unwelcome attention from Romans, Saxons, Danes and Normans. These lively fellows apparently found it ideal for the Number 1 sport of those times: Murder, Rape and Pillage. Once the country was more or less unified under one tyrant's thumb, and the old sport gave way to more sophisticated ways of making life unpleasant for other people, East Anglia gradually dropped out of the popularity charts.

In the first place it was, and is, flat; not a decent sized hill anywhere and no rock to use in banging up a really worthwhile castle. The medieval lord, despot or whatever never really felt happy unless he was in hilly country, it was so much more interesting for fighting in and you could see your enemy coming. Not like the tedious flat stretches of forest, heath and marsh that characterised East Anglia, where armies could miss each other in the wilderness. The second point of disfavour held that it was so darned cold. All right when there was plenty of murder, rape and pillage to keep you warm, but no place for practising the less energetic pastimes of poisoning, garrotting and red hot poker slipping as taken up by England's royalty and hangers on in the middle ages.

So everyone who was anyone in the social order of the times went west, leaving the rude peasants to the icy North Sea winds that so frequently chilled the eastern counties. From then on East Anglia was regarded as one of the most lugubrious spots in Britain, a place you might talk about but where, if you had any aspirations at all, you would never choose to live. Norfolk and Suffolk were way-out wildernesses hemmed in by Cambridgeshire, which was then little more than a bog. Even Essex, bang on the capital's doorstep, was fit only for a spot of deerhunting and serf-snatching.

This general disdain for the eastern counties continued right up until the second half of the 20th century. Then their whole status was suddenly changed by Britain's decision to prostrate itself before the commerce of Europe. During the intervening eight or nine hundred years the British tribes had been so successful in the art of carving up the countryside – and each other in the process – that they had extended their ranging world-wide. In fact, they became quite carried away with smash-and-grab tactics, expending quite a lot of effort, to say nothing of blood, adding to their portfolio of acquisitions places that, in comparison, made East Anglia look like the Garden of Eden. Having made a champion job of upsetting the human applecart all round the globe, decadency suddenly set in. This took the form of an ever accelerating self-denigration, despite having given all the other tribes a blueprint for industry and an international language.

Having divested themselves of an empire, the next step in national self-flagellation was to suffer remorse for being the *agent provocateur* of Europe, a role played quite successfully since 1066. To ingratiate themselves, the British joined Europe's very uncommon market. It was this move that brought about the great East Anglian revival.

The proximity of the Essex-Suffolk-Norfolk bulge to the continent made it an ideal place in which to develop great ports out of little seaside towns, the better to ship in all the goodies. This in turn made a need for warehouses, storage and distribution facilities, better communications and, of course, more people to handle the work. With the people came houses, Tescos, Chinese take-aways and private shops. The place was commercially booming.

It would be wrong to credit the changed standing of East Anglia solely to Euro-worship. The fashionable and warmer places in England had become so over-subscribed and expensive by the years following the tussel with Adolph Hitler, that those whose work or business lay in the metropolis began to look elsewhere for homes. Neglected East Anglia was the obvious place and proved ideal commuting country. The cold winds still whipped over the North Sea from Siberia, but now everyone could be protected from the elements by that mechanical cocoon, the motor car. Undoubtedly the supreme 20th-century vice, the car also allowed easy access to the remotest corners of the region. Offshoots of the automobile, the tractor and the bulldozer, had already enabled many power-happy farmers to open up the flat landscape still further, thus opening up the view so that the newcomers could comfortably see the next new housing development from their own.

So what do the original natives think of all this? Not that there are, proportionately, many of them left. Generally there is a stoic acceptance, together with the well tested attitude that if you can't beat 'em, join 'em. Most are quite happy to muscle in on anything that's going. Not that the newcomers are really much trouble once out of their cars. The majority are quite happy at home indoors, paying homage to the television set and receiving another dose of indoctrination on how ghastly the British are and have been.

You may further ask what have the East Anglians been up to in the centuries of neglect before the recent upturn? The answer is agriculture. They hacked down their oak forests to provide tim-bers for the ships used by fellow countrymen to go buccaneering around the globe and turned into farmland the rich soil they uncovered. Throughout these years the peasantry also provided a goodly share of the cannon fodder for various military enterprises, but mostly they followed the plough, milked the cow and fed the sow. Generally quiet and unassuming fellows, they were not without initiative when they saw an opportunity to get on to a good thing. Thus a few sailed a little ship out of Ipswich in 1606 to get the very first settler's foot into the American colonies.

With the surge of industry elsewhere in Britain during the 19th century, coupled with the surge in population, the good farmlands of East Anglia came into their own. However, the demand for food was short-lived. The products that Britain's industry sold abroad brought back cheaper food than ever the East Anglian farmer or his men could grow. Thereafter rural prosperity yo-yoed – for, like soldiers, farmers were valuable only in times of war. Bonaparte's threat demonstrated this and so did the Kaiser's. By the 1920s British farming was heading for the worst depression yet.

I arrived on this scene in the late 1920s, but my early memories of the hamlet where my parents' farm was situated do not reflect the agricultural impoverishment of the times. I was insulated from that knowledge by my childhood ignorance. For the labourers and artisans life was hard but uncomplicated, much the same as it had been for centuries. Our family was privileged in having a second-hand car and a telephone, but many who lived in the cluster of cottages did not even own a bicycle. Several families still drew their water by bucket from a spring. Electricity had not yet arrived. Rabbits provided the staple meat; every household kept hens and many had a pig in the back garden, fed on kitchen scraps. The average cottager could almost live off his garden and the countryside. It was a frugal existence, though. A few pints of mild and bitter and a packet or two of Woodbines each week were the greatest luxuries that most men could afford.

The depressed state of farming in the Twenties and Thirties saw many bankruptcies. Survival hinged on producing food which could not easily be imported from abroad because of deterioration. Milk, eggs, poultry, fresh fruit and vegetables became the principal lifelines. With difficulty my father survived with a dairy herd and a retail milk round. Much arable land lay derelict simply because it did not pay to farm.

Various machines introduced in the latter part of the 19th

century took some of the backache out of farming operations, but most of them were intended to speed up work rather than save labour and even by the 1930s tractors were few and the horse still the motive power on the land. Tractor fuel cost money while horses could be maintained on a farm pasture and homegrown oats and hay.

All this was to change rapidly when the Nazi blitzkrieg swept across Europe and the U-boats threatened merchant shipping. The plough came back into favour, retrieved from the nettles where it had reposed since the last spot of bother with the Germans. In those war years everything that could be tilled was tilled as the nation again faced possible starvation. For the most part the equipment used was similar to – and sometimes the same as – that used in the First World War and the methods were still labour intensive. From 1939 to 1945, and during the immediate post-war years, cereals were still cut with a binder and the resulting sheaves pitched and stacked to await separation of the grain by a contractor's thrashing tackle. Sugar beet were loosened in the soil with a special plough, pulled, shaken and laid in rows by hand. Then the leaves and crowns were removed with a topping knife and the roots forked into a cart for transport to a clamp. Other arable crops were just as demanding of human effort. However, some new labour-saving equipment from America, which reached British farms during the war, pointed the way to a much easier lot for those who worked the land.

Instead of reverting to depression status, British agriculture survived and prospered through the next four decades. The Empire was gone, the nation was in the poorhouse and disinclined to spend on the purchase of food from overseas – even if it had been cheaply available. So successive governments encouraged the farmer to grow more and use the new technology. Combine harvesters arrived, eventually turning the job of gathering grain into one conducted from a comfie seat in a dust-free cab. Sugar-beet harvesters banished that back-breaking task, and hydraulic muscle replaced many of the manual lifting jobs. Machines which could far outpace man and horse soon eliminated the latter completely and reduced the numbers of the former severely. On our farm the peak of 12 employees in 1946 had been reduced to just two 40 years later. The last carthorse went in 1950.

There were other factors that made arable farming less arduous, more efficient and more productive in the second half of the century. The farmer now had concentrated fertilisers to promote growth, fungicides to alleviate plant diseases and, probably the most significant, herbicides to eliminate the really competitive weeds. In the old days weeds had been controlled primarily by hand and hoe, or by the expensive procedure of fallowing a field for a year while frequently moving the surface to kill any plant growth. New strains and varieties of the major crops were yet another considerable aid to better yields.

In short, the engineers, chemists and scientists had done most to effect the remarkable change in agriculture. From the position in the 1940s when British agriculture did not provide half our temperate food requirements, to that in the 1980s when most sections of the industry were producing surpluses, we never had it so good. Even so, farming profitability was never easy, successive governments saw to that. Keeping the nation's belly full may be of primary importance to government, but so is the cost. Unlike most other industries, where a percentage for profit is tacked on to production costs, agriculture has to take whatever is the going rate in a market place artificially manipulated by politicians.

What of the men who worked the land? In my youth, when numbers were needed, they were the core of any rural village community. And in the true rural village most other occupations were connected with sustaining the requirements of farm workers and farm ancillary trades. In those days, when motor cars were comparatively few and public transport sparse, villagers did not venture far afield; they generally had no need to. Each village was then much more an introverted community, in many respects self-sufficient. In consequence folk two miles down the road tended to be looked upon as foreigners.

During my childhood, only Wully and Rue worked regularly on this farm, with an occasional hand from the venerable Horrie.

Wully was cowman and Rue turned his hand to just about any-thing. Neither was young – to me. Both had first seen the light of day before the 20th century dawned. Horrie could give them 20 years more; he was over 70. With the outbreak of war the labour force increased dramatically. The energetic Archie was recruited to become chief horseman. Up to that time he had associated with horses all his working life. He was in his early thirties then and one would have thought still young enough to learn new tricks. But somehow he never really got the hang of using tractors. He drove them for many years, right up until he retired, yet never found the right philosophy for working with the iron beasts.

Wully, who reckoned he was getting too stiff for bending under cows, graduated to second horseman in the war years and then on to tractors. The herd was taken over by the stringy Clive, again at 45 no youngster; but then most of the young men were away at war. Clive was a foreigner to the rest of the farm, a foreigner not from the next village but from Welsh Wales. He had a wife even skinnier than himself who had, however, an enormous bust. Wully and Rue, who had those sort of minds, seemed quite mesmerised by this woman. If she happened by, they would 'garp' at her and pretend that her breasts incomprehensibly defied the laws of gravity.

As labour was so scarce the Guv'nor enlisted the part-time services of several old boys who had retired and of others such as roadmen and carpenters, who came to lend a hand during the long summer evenings or weekends. Then came the Land Army girls; young women who had been recruited to fill the vacancies on the farms. They came from all over the country and from all walks of life. Some were excellent, taking to agriculture despite the hard and often dirty work; the majority, however, succumbed to something or other pretty quickly and departed. The turnover was fairly rapid, the girls and their problems putting years on the Guv'nor – or so he professed. The dearth of labour caused the Gov'nor to employ a few characters who in more normal times he would never have entertained. One was Nasty, well known as a rogue who had pulled many a fast one in the area. His crimes were

fairly petty and often involved women who were easily taken in by his handsome countenance and glib tongue. Nasty was in his thirties when he was employed on the farm, although from my memory there was not much work attached to the employment. He lasted only a couple of years or so until he found easier gain.

In the years following hostilities the Land Army girls soon left the scene and the labour force swelled with men just out of the forces, Italian ex-POWs and even Wernie, one-time member of the Wermacht, who put everyone else to shame when it came to physical effort. Most of these newcomers were itinerant and soon on their way to better-paying jobs outside agriculture. By the early Fifties two or three youngsters had joined the fold, including Tim and Toby from local village homes. Thereafter, as mechanisation and new farming techniques took hold, so, through natural wastage, the labour force declined. The Guv'nor died in the early Sixties. Rue and Archie retired in the Seventies, and since then the only working feet on this land have been Tim's, Toby's and my own. For that matter a parish of 400 souls which once rated 27 farmers and smallholders now has eight. And, at a guess, about a hundred farm workers have been reduced to fewer than a score. The hamlet where I lived as a boy is completely devoid of labourers and artisans. Instead, the cottages are home to retired folk and commuters. The 12 miles to the big town or five to the nearest station are but a dawdle away in a car. The whole character of the place has changed, not necessarily for the worse. Meagre dwellings have been renovated and so improved internally as to be beyond recognition to the occupants of a half century ago; they now have central heating, double glazing and all the delights of present-day living.

The character of the whole village has changed, too. Once centred upon local agriculture, it is now largely a dormitory for those who work elsewhere and who find it a more desirable place to live than Suburbia. Inevitably, as the newcomers have become numerically dominant, their attitudes and values have come into prominence. They tend to see the countryside in romantic and leisure terms, as a rural pleasure park for their enjoyment rather than as a food factory where man wrestles with nature. Footpaths have become nice places on which to take doggy for a walk rather than short cuts to the pub or place of work. Hedgerows are pretty things to look at, shelters for wildlife; not the source of popguns, catapult crotches, clothes pegs, linen props and the many other things they were to the countryman early this century.

There is but one element in this social change that really annoys me; the patronising view of country folk expressed by some newcomers, particularly the more academically inclined. Rather as 19th century explorers of darkest Africa sent back anthropological reports on the natives, so many self-appointed social commentators from the new East Anglian occupation held forth in condescending fashion on the observed manner of the peasantry. It would not have been so bad had they recognised the humour that thrives among the original inhabitants. Instead these blinkered sociologists often portrayed the farm worker as a pitiful serf.

I have never known a true farm worker who did not possess a strong, if reserved, pride; and most had a good sense of humour, often dry, often subtle. It was most notable in the old men – those in their seventies and eighties in whose lifetime the pattern of centuries has been banished for ever. Perhaps the close village communities of days gone by provided a greater store of material. Not much could be kept secret and gossip was a major cottage industry. Perhaps also, they had more time to reminisce than younger generations. Somehow I do not think the current social environment will produce the characters and rich stories of the past. Some of these stories follow and, for good measure, I have thrown in a few memories of my own.

The Iron Horse

The layout of the parish in which I farm is a bit like half a wagon wheel. The boundary follows a more or less straight line along the river, then curves round in a wide semicircle out of the valley and back again to meet the river three miles further along. The village street with its cluster of shops, houses and places of worship forms the hub at the riverside, while country lanes, like convoluted spokes, radiate out towards the parish boundary. Between the lanes lies a typical English hotch-potch of fields, woods, farm-steads and the odd gentlefolk's residence, together with less attractive features such as the sewage works and a used car dump. This not untypical patch of rural Suffolk has developed over the centuries without any apparent attention to orderliness. The rationale behind the situation of buildings and the shapes of fields is beyond my understanding, possibly because there was no rationale involved.

Many of the farmhouses are now simply private residences, their lands having been sold away to neighbours. Most of this farm wastage that has taken place since the Second World War involved the small acreage places which have not been favoured by economic trends. In my youth there must have been a score of holdings that ran to between two and twenty acres. All have now gone. They were worked, administered or jollied along by a rich variety of characters who had at least one thing in common, they were, in their different ways, extremely wily; possibly a necessary quality in anyone who survived the agricultural depression of the Thirties.

There were extremes in their craftiness just as in their farming activity. The indolent Harry Newson, who had a couple of acres behind his cottage, went through all the motions just to obtain an agricultural rating and secure other benefits from the State, but the only farming use his land was put to was to be grazed by somebody else's cattle. At the other extreme was the industrious widow, Mrs Maggs, who never seemed to rest from toil on her four-acre holding. Nevertheless her efficiency did not extend to the repair of fences, for on more than one occasion her Jersey cow 'escaped' into the adjoining meadow to obtain service from the Guv'nor's bull, free of charge. Most of these folk were likeable and kindly, even if you did have to keep your wits about you in any dealing with them. There was, however, one individual I could never warm to.

Mr Fulger had a smallholding that butted on to the far end of our Fifteen Acres, a level rectangular field bounded by hedgerows stiffened with many pollarded elms. It seemed that whenever I had some cultivation task to perform in that field, Fulger would appear to inspect and comment. I was the only recipient of his attention, most probably because I had been reared to be tolerant and polite. Had Fulger made inspections and comments on the work of Rue, Wully or Archie he would no doubt have been quickly told to 'bugger off'. The trouble was that I found Fulger's interest in my work quite unsettling because of the way he went about it. For example, if I was ploughing he would appear from a gap in his hedge when I was at the far end of the field. He would then squat and eye up the furrow to see if it was straight or, alternatively, produce a pocket rule and plumb the depth in one or two places. By the time I had driven tractor and plough back up the furrow he would have disappeared. He would repeat this routine perhaps two or three times a day. Sometimes I would see him shaking his head before disappearing back through the gap in the hedge. The psychological effect of his actions was to have me worrying that I was not ploughing a constant depth or a straight furrow.

Mr Fulger's prime obsession was with what he called 'moulds'. If I was harrowing or drilling seed he would soon appear to pick up a handful of soil or drag a boot through the surface before gesticulating for me to stop the tractor. 'You ain't goin' to do no good here', he would say. 'You ain't got no moulds.' 'Mould', I should explain, is another name for tilth, that fine crumby condition of the soil that promotes the establishment of plant life and is desirable for seeding. Moulds can best be achieved by weathering action, particularly frosts, the passage of harrows and the like over the soil being no match for the powers of nature.

A fine tilth is certainly important in ensuring a good start for a crop. To Fulger it was apparently the be-all and end-all of successful husbandry, judging by the number of times he lectured me on the subject. I received a regular earful one year when we had sugar beet on the Fifteen Acres and growth was patchy. Whenever I was working there Fulger would appear, sometimes to carry out his inspections when I was at the other end of the field, or, more often, to pounce upon me from the hedge shouting, 'You wouldn't have this mess if you'd got proper moulds.'

Apart from the question of courtesy, Fulger could not be ignored because he did know what he was talking about, having farmed quite extensively himself in past years. My understanding is that he sold up during the depression, using the proceeds to buy the seven-acre field above our Fifteen Acres and build a bungalow. On this smallholding he grew a variety of vegetables and several sorts of garden flowers for their seeds. He was quite industrious and did all the work himself with the aid of what was then termed a 'horticultural tractor'. It was known as the Iron Horse, but whether this was its proprietary name or simply the name bestowed upon it by Fulger, I cannot recall. In configuration it consisted of two lugged steel drive wheels between which reposed the transmission and a ten-horsepower engine. Two long handles projecting rearwards provided the means by which an operator, walking behind, steered the beast. A single-furrow plough, or any one of a number of other implements, could be attached aft of the wheels. This machine was not easy to master and required considerable strength to steer, particularly over rough ground. I saw it lift Fulger off his feet on more than one occasion as it twisted and lurched across ploughed land. Fulger treated this inanimate brute like an errant horse, thumping on the fuel tank and cursing whenever it failed to perform as required. The extent of his invective was rarely to be heard because the engine made such a hell of a din.

As I have made plain, I did not like Mr Fulger and would have preferred to avoid his criticisms. There was, however, one re-deeming factor associated with Fulger and that was his daughter. June Fulger was described by my mother as 'a fine figure of a woman' and by Wully as 'a grut ole gal'. In truth the delectable June was well proportioned, being around five feet ten inches tall and fully curved to match her height. She was undeniably pretty, with a bright countenance and long brunette hair. In build and features she was quite unlike the short, wiry Fulger and his mousey wife. Indeed it was rumoured, but never confirmed to my know-ledge, that June was adopted.

She and I were both the same age – at the time of which I tell, 19 – but where I was reserved and self-conscious, June was much more assured and worldly. She worked in a bank in Ipswich and I rarely had the opportunity of saying more than 'Hello' to her as she pedalled to catch the bus each morning. I was certainly not the only young fellow who aspired to closer acquaintance with this attrac-tive young lady, although it seemed she was just as elusive to others. Unfortunately, Wully sensed my interest when she cycled past one day. As was to be expected he rather spoilt my romantic notions with his uncouth pronouncement: 'Boy, you wanta keep away from her. If she get her grut legs wrapped round you, you'll be in proper trouble!'

It transpired that my interest in June was soon revived. That year we grew sugar beet on the Fifteen Acres, and I spent many long days with a tractor and inter-row hoe slowly driving back and forth moving the topsoil to prevent the growth of weeds. Periodi-cally the tractor's sparking plugs would soot up and I would have to take them out and clean them. On one occasion this happened at Fulger's end of the field and a movement from the gap in the hedge brought my eyes up to feast on the pleasant sight of June. She gave

me an unnerving smile: 'Father says would you like to come and
have a cup of tea?'

Had the invitation come directly from Fulger himself I would
have found some excuse to decline, but in the circumstances there
was no way I would refuse. Following in June's wake through the
rows of red and gold flowers towards Fulger's bungalow, I was
too tongue-tied to strike up a conversation with her. She instigated
what little dialogue we had.

'How's your mother?'

'All right thanks.'

'Haven't seen your brother lately, how's he getting on?'

'All right thanks.'

And so on.

For once Mr Fulger didn't take me to task over farming operations, instead he showed interest in the plug-fouling problems
with my tractor. This was something that I could be voluble
about, even though June was hovering in the background. Fulger
mentioned the difficulty he sometimes had in starting his Iron
Horse: did I think it was plugs? Not likely, I advised, as it ran on
petrol, not vaporising oil. More probably the magneto. Would I
have a look at the magneto? Yes, I'd have a peep. It was full of dirt
and oil. Then I saw my opening. I could not stop now in the
Guv'nor's time, but if it would be helpful I would come round
after work and clean the magneto for him. Yes, he'd be most
grateful.

Thus began an exciting development in my young life. For I had
soon ingratiated myself with the Fulgers through demonstrating
mechanical knowledge and aptitude. Over the next few weeks I
not only refurbished the Iron Horse's magneto but replaced two
wheel bearings for Fulger and tuned up the carburettor. I even got
to readjusting the Sturmey-Archer three-speed gear on June's
bike. I was rewarded with innumerable cups of tea and several
hunks of cake, but these were as nothing against the opportunities I
had of exchanging a few words with the alluring June. To prolong
the association, I diagnosed that the Iron Horse was in need of a
cylinder rebore and could not be expected to regain performance

or stop burning lubricating oil until it had had a major overhaul. It was agreed that I would dismantle the engine and, when Mr Fulger obtained the necessary parts and had had the cylinder relined, reassemble it. While the details were gone over I could hardly keep my eyes off June, whose summer blouse revealed a quite daring amount of cleavage for those days. Oh yes, things were progressing nicely.

The facts were that I had underestimated the difficulty of reconditioning the Iron Horse's engine. It did not take long to remove; putting it back was a different matter and required a whole week of evenings. Mr Fulger showed signs of impatience and probably thought I was never going to get the thing together. On one occasion I got a little finger jammed in a gear and well and truly bloodied. The pain seemed worthwhile though, when June was despatched from the bungalow to administer to me with hot water, iodine and bandage, particularly as she still had that tantalising blouse on. Each abrupt movement quite unnerved me; I think I went around in a stupor all next day.

Thankfully, on completion of its overhaul the Iron Horse sprang to life after the first two or three tugs of the starting handle. Mr Fulger actually grinned with delight, the only time I had seen him display such an emotion. June put her arm around my shoulders and gave me a hug, saying, 'Well done, well done.' I was in ecstasy.

My starry-eyed disposition must have been noticed at home because I was being teased. I fantasized about marriage – a daydream marred only by the thought of Mr Fulger as a father-in-law. Eventually, I even came to terms with that. I sought some new reason to call on the Fulgers, and finally hit upon the need to check the Iron Horse's engine to see if any final adjustments were required.

Mr Fulger was most affable, even more so than when the rejuvenated Iron Horse burst into life. Yes, he said, it was running very well. Nowhere near the trouble to start that it had been. I checked the engine over and pronounced all to be fine. At this stage I expected to be asked in for the usual cuppa. Instead, my world crashed around my dreams. 'Well, I must get along in,' Mr Fulger called as he trotted away towards the bungalow, 'Got to get changed to go to June's engagement party.'

Youth takes such experiences most sorely to heart, but in the following days I put on a brave face. Even when someone volunteered that June Fulger was engaged to a bank clerk, I nonchalantly pretended that it was old news. Gradually, as the emotional fog cleared, my hurt turned to anger and humiliation. The truth was that in all those visits I really hadn't been much in June's company at all. She rarely came near me, except to dispense tea and cakes. If there had been any mutual attraction she would surely have come out to watch my struggles with the Iron Horse, ready to counsel and coax. Apart from the start-up night she hadn't appeared of her own volition. Tea, cake and bandages had all come at father's command. We'd still never had any really worthwhile conversation. Such was my infatuation that I had been blinded by my own fantasies. The more I thought about it, the clearer it became. Fulger's Iron Horse had received a complete overhaul for no more than the cost of the parts and refreshment for the mechanic! Further, I now suspected June had connived in this enterprise.

A week or two later the knife was turned in the wound. Into the farmyard came one of the local tractor salesmen for a Colchester-based tractor dealer. His eyes lit up when he saw me. 'Must say you're quite the budding engineer,' he patronised, 'Did a remarkably fine job with that old Iron Horse of Mr Fulger's. He wanted to trade it in last month for a new little Ferguson but I told him I couldn't allow him much while it was in that state. Tricky things to overhaul and costly too because they're so fiddly. You can't sell them unless they're in good nick so I'd never have been able to shift it if he hadn't got you to do it up. Hope he paid you well?' He never got an answer; only a forced laugh. I was speechless.

Mr Fulger took delivery of his little grey Ferguson that week. Every time I saw him on it going up and down his rows of red and yellow flowers I hoped the thing would blow up. It never did. Occasionally he still hopped through the gap in the hedge to go on about moulds but whenever I could I pretended not to see him.

The nerve of the man; or did he think I never cottoned on to his rotten game. Of course, it's all a laugh now. Still, I don't think I have ever been taken to the cleaners quite so effectively.

The voluptuous June married her bank clerk and probably lived happily ever after. Someone told me that she grew fat in middle age – though it sounds like sour grapes to mention it here. Her husband eventually became a branch manager in one of the 'Big Four' banks. I've never done business there as a matter of principle. As for Mr Fulger, he's been in the churchyard for years. Mouldering I dare say.

The Sporting Postman

Whenever I go to post a letter in the local box there is a good chance that I shall be waylaid by old Mr Newson. The pillar box stands just outside his garden fence and provides him with excellent opportunities for striking up conversations with folk posting letters. 'Conversations', though, is hardly the right word, for old Newson is adept at quickly becoming the speaker and making the other party the listener. He delights in reminiscences, the only problem being that one is never quite sure if there is more to it than he is telling, or if he is telling more than there is to it.

To illustrate my point, I was popping a letter in the box when old Newson called out: 'Cost something to send a letter now don't it?'

'Certainly does,' I replied.

'Time was when it were only a penny h'penny – and that were real money. Mind you, the posties is better paid than they was and I think the old boys ought to get more than they do. Rough old job pushin' them bikes around.' Old, when applied to the postmen, is a term of endearment. Mr Newson is old enough to be the father of both our locals. 'They earn their keep,' he continued. 'Not like them telephone gangs what sit around in lorries playin' cards while the posties is out in the wet. I used to be a postman myself once. Time I lived down the other side of Maldon, afore the war that were. Not many folk around the marshes in them days.

'I had to bike ten mile a day I reckon to get to all the houses – and there were two of us to do it, too. The other feller – Charlie – well, I don't remember his last name but his first was Charlie. He was a rum beggar. Used to do a bit of poachin' while he was on his rounds.

'Carried an old Betty ferret and a few nets in his bag, and when he was gettin' a bit tired of pushin' his old bike he'd down with it and pop the ferret into a burrow. Be an hour sometimes, but there weren't many people about early in the mornin', and it was that lonely around here nobody ever missed him. Did quite well – his bag were often heavier when he come back than when he went out.'

'Enterprising,' I said.

'Yes,' said Mr Newson. 'The only trouble was the ferret. Well, you know how they pong. Worse than an old goat. Course, he was so used to it he didn't notice; like it is with any smell you're with long enough. People who didn't know about the ferret thought it was him. Cor, some of 'em must a thought the job was ruinin' his feet. Worse still, all the letters used to stink, bein' in the next compartment to the ferret. People round there was always gettin' stinkin' letters from people!'

Old Newson was briefly convulsed with laughter at his own joke. Then, after dabbing his mouth with a spotless white handkerchief, he went on: 'What brought things to a head was one Christmas when somebody sent the vicar's wife a packet of bath salts for a present and Charlie accidentally put it in with the ferret. You can imagine what she thought when she found that lot on her mat. Ah, but the vicar weren't no fool, not he. He'd had a whiff of ferret before somewhere. Went stormin' into the post office and played up merry hell he did.'

'Did Charlie get the sack?' I enquired.

'No, the postmaster didn't know what was goin' on, and after that Charlie used to carry the ferret in his coat pocket. Mind you he come unstuck in the end. Got a bit darin' and put the ferret down a burrow in somebody's garden hedge early one mornin'. That came out of a hole the other side he hadn't netted and started runnin' about the garden. So over he goes to get it, but the darn thing run under the door of a privy. Well, Charlie's just comin' out after pickin' up his ferret when some old gal comes trottin' down the garden path.

' "Sorry, missus," he says. "I got took short." Quick thinkin' fellow, our Charlie. You got to hand it to him. He'd ha' got away with it only he'd put the ferret in his pocket so the old gal shouldn't see it. Bein' a bit nervous he must have had hold of it too hard. Anyway the ferret took a great lump out of the little finger of his left hand. Charlie wholly shruck and called that ferret a few choice things. Only the old gal thought he was swearing at her. Course, he got the sack.'

The curious thing is that I've seen an old scar on the little finger of Mr Newson's left hand. When questioned about it he makes evasive answers. Curious.

The Biter

Some people look upon horses as the height of pleasure, a delight beyond compare. This is one vice I will never get hooked on. For me the horse is a smelly and treacherous monster, to be approached with as much trepidation as one reserves for a crocodile. This ingrained mixture of hate and fear stems from youthful experiences of being pushed, pummelled, dragged, squashed, bitten and dribbled on by the brutes, all in the course of trying to persuade them to contribute motive power to whatever was attached behind. My approach was always one of gentleness and benevolence, a consideration that they did not hesitate to abuse.

The most despicable was a Suffolk gelding, whose true name I cannot recall, but which left its mark on my person both physically and mentally as The Biter. Perhaps this desire to bite was retaliation for the injustice perpetrated upon it by man.

My association with The Biter reached its climax one hot June day when we were sent to horse-hoe sugar beet with old Wully. Wully was a smallish man, strong of arm but – as his wife neatly put it – 'a bit weak on his pins'. He always held that long years spent as a cowman, squatting under udders, was the cause of his being bow-legged and flat-footed.

Be that as it may, Wully was never one to walk any further than he could possibly help. Plodding behind a steerage hoe was not a job he would have selected for himself, any more than he would have picked me to lead the horse. The combination and situation

brought friction that mounted as the sun burned higher into the sky.

'To yer! From yer! To yer! Whoooo! Where do you think yer a goin'? Ya bloody near in the next row,' Old Wully would yell.

'It's the horse. It keeps wrenching its head about. I can hardly hold it.'

'Course that'll wrench its head if yer hold it like that. Git hold o' the bridle aginst the bit.'

His unflattering stream of obscenities did little to smooth the path of progress. The culmination of the morning's activities came near lunch when, in an unguarded moment, the wretched animal sank its nasty yellow teeth into my hair, almost scalping me.

'It ain't no good you sendin' that boy with me agin. He couldn't lead a starvin' cow to a bucket of oats. He's wuss than hopeless,' Wully told the Guv'nor. So I was relegated to other tasks while Vicky, a somewhat buxom Army girl, was despatched to lead the horse for Wully.

But that threesome was soon in trouble, too. Vicky unwisely released her grip on The Biter when the team halted for Wully to make an adjustment to the hoe. In a flash The Biter had a mouthful of WLA issue shirt, shredding it right across the back and snapping a bra strap as well.

It was a tearful and dishevelled girl who arrived in the farmyard first to inform the Guv'nor that she refused to handle 'that horse' again. Some ten minutes elapsed before Wully arrived. 'Weren't goin' to come along the road with her. People might think I done it,' he confided, seriously.

The Guv'nor sold The Biter a few days later, much to Wully's chagrin. 'Darn fool. That was a good hoss. He alus was soft with women.'

As for Vicky, she obviously decided farm life was too hazardous a way to see out the war, for following this incident she gave the Guv'nor notice and left to join one of the women's services. Vicky is probably a grandmother now, but I bet she hasn't forgotten her Land Army days. After all, there can't be many women who can claim to have been ravished by a horse.

Them Furriners

Nobody, not anyone, tells William Rupert Scrutts what to do. You can suggest that the mangel need hoeing, hint that the men could do with a hand riddling potatoes, casually mention that the hedge along Friar's Lane needs trimming back, but you never never command Ol' Rue to do anything – if you want him to do it.

And that is the way it has been for as long as I can remember – which is now far too long.

Ol' Rue was Ol' Rue 40 years ago and doesn't really seem to have changed at all. Short, arched, beady eyed, two-days' stubble growth, collarless shirt and cloth cap were familiar features then as now. Somewhere, sometime he must have retired but I cannot tell you when, and he could now be anything from 75 to knocking the century.

Ask him outright; 'How old are you Rue?' and the reply will be; 'Old 'nough to know better than answer a darn silly question like that!' Ask him craftily; 'Now let me see, you retired the year the Queen married didn't you Rue?' and the response will be; 'I ain't retirin' till they carry me in the Co-op hearse.'

You will gather that Ol' Rue is, to say the least, a very independent character. Thus, when he regularly appears for a day or so on the farm it is he who decides what he is going to do. Don't misunderstand me. He doesn't pick the easy jobs, in fact he'll still tackle tasks a man 50 years his junior would flinch from. It is simply that he doesn't like to do anything that is put to him as a direct request. 'Just bloody awkwardness' is how the others sum up Ol' Rue behind his back, but everyone humours him to his face. It has always been like that.

Ol' Rue has strong feelings on a lot of matters. Currently the quality and price of the liquid sold at his local as beer (which he insists comes from gnats); the silhouette of dancing girls on telly (which troubles his blood pressure); and Furriners (who shouldn't exist).

It is the latter which seem to be of most concern, particularly with the advent of the Common Market, although Ol' Rue has been preoccupied with furriners for as long as I can remember.

Forty years ago a furriner was anyone not born and bred in this parish or those that surround it. A man from two parishes away was an alien. I once heard Ol' Rue passing acid comment on a fellow who had lost his way and just cycled off after asking us directions. 'He's one of them Grut Wenham clod-heads. He wouldn't know where he was goin' in his marriage bed! But what can you expect from furriners!' This I thought was a bit unfair as there happened to be a very dense November fog at the time. Ol' Rue didn't really come into contact with many furriners until the 1940s because about the longest journey he ever appears to have made was from his house to a pub – and as there were six of those within a mile there was little chance of him wandering further afield.

With such hostility towards those who lived but a few miles away, it can be appreciated that when real furriners appeared in our village during the last war, this was far more troubling to Ol' Rue than any of Hitler's bombs, even though the furriners were supposed to be our allies. Matters were not helped when his youngest daughter became a bit too free with the Free French or when an American jeep failed to take the bend outside his house, knocked down his garden fence, three rows of runner beans, squashed his prize marrow and put his hens off the lay for a week. He never forgot the details of destruction even though he was more than amply compensated by the American authorities.

But what really hardened him against all furriners was the

behaviour of the then enemy. We had some German prisoners of war to help with haymaking in the year following the cessation of hostilities. Two of these, great strong chaps, all brawn and muscle, were delegated to pitch loose hay on to a cart where Ol' Rue was to load it and I was to be loader's boy. The pitchers took a little while to get the hang of using the forks, but once in their stride the hay came up fast and in gigantic forkfuls, almost a hay-cock at one time. It was more than Ol' Rue could comfortably deal with and he soon demanded that the pitchers slacken the pace. Unfortunately the Germans' command of English wasn't very good and they obviously didn't understand or appreciate Ol' Rue's forceful oaths of protest. The great forkfuls kept coming and it was all we could do to prevent ourselves being buried under them, let alone place them. This was too much for Ol' Rue who, shaking with anger and uttering a torrent of abuse, slid off the load and went stomping away across the field. The Germans at first seemed a bit mystified by his action. Then one man's face lit up with understanding. 'Jetzt ich verstehe', he said, turning to me. 'He go to quickly water make, ja?'

A further hardening of Ol' Rue's contempt for furriners occurred in the late 1950s as the result of our taking on student help at harvest time. The two young men sent along by a local youth organisation were Italian holiday exchange students. One was a true Adonis who appeared to have all the physical equipment for moving straw bales but was very loath to use it. He had the disturbing habit of casting off his clothing at the first shaft of sunlight and going about in nothing more than an extremely brief pair of red swimming trunks and rope sandals. Moreover, he seemed to spend the best part of his time flexing his body beautiful and admiring himself. Periodically he would make some Italian exclamation of delight, stretching out his arms and twisting his brown torso while watching his muscles ripple with obvious self-adulation.

Ol' Rue didn't say a lot, he didn't have to, the look on his face was enough. In any case he was far more troubled by the other Italian, a short swarthy lad with an extremely melodious voice.

There was no denying the quality of his vocal cords, the trouble was that he seemed able to render only one melody, part of *La Boheme*. Throughout the day he would erupt into this operatic performance which, pleasant for the first few occasions, began to pall after a dozen times. After three days Ol' Rue informed us that he had found another pressing job on the farm. ' 'Course if I stays along of that Iti' gramaphone with a stuck needle I'll break his bloody record, beggered if I don't!'

In recent years Ol' Rue has been more troubled by what he has read in the papers about foreign immigration to Britain than by personal experience. As mentioned previously, our membership of the E.E.C. had always caused him some concern. Matters came to a head one spring day when I beheld our Rue bearing down on me with obvious signs of displeasure. 'Is that right you're havin' a student to work here this harvest?' he began. I knew what con- cerned him. 'Yes, but he's English,' I consoled.

'He better be, otherwise I ain't comin' to work I can tell yer', he threatened. 'Just because of this Common Market you needn't be thinking you'll have any of those wogs on the place or I'm off for one,' he said, warming to the tirade.

'Wogs?' I queried.

'Well, white wogs then – and they're the worst kind 'cause you can't alus tell they're wogs. At least when you sees one of them coloured uns coming down the road you can cross over the other side to get out of their way. That Unoch Powell is right. All the beggers want sending home.'

'Enoch Powell,' I corrected, but Ol' Rue was not to be checked.

'He don't want to get us mixed up with that Common Market and let all those wogs in here, not Unoch Powell. I seen enough of them wogs already. Look what a good for nothin' lot them French soldiers were we had round here in the war. Remember 'em? (I remembered and I'm sure his daughter does too) and them damn Jerry prisoners, and as for that pansy Italian what ran around good as naked, likes of him arn't fit to mix with decent people.'

It took several minutes for Ol' Rue to get this out of his system and I was finally able to cajole him into believing that I sympath-

ised with his views. There the matter would have rested but for an incident that occurred later in that summer.

On one of those very rare occasions when one could claim it was a really hot day, I was walking through the farmyard when the unmistakable odour of freshly turned manure asserted itself. Curious, I investigated and was amazed to see the occasional forkful of muck sailing out of an empty calf-box doorway. Delivery was admittedly intermittent – several flying forkfuls and then nothing for a minute or more. While mucking out a calf box may be a good task for a bitterly cold winter's day, it is not the sort of job for the hottest helping of sunlight of the summer. I would never dream of asking anyone to throw out muck on a hot day and the thought that someone was actually doing it of their own volition left me incredulous. There had to be some extraordinary reason – and there was!

Looking in the door I beheld the hunched figure of Ol' Rue, his face turned towards the back wall. He was peering through a knot hole in the weatherboarding and, judging by his expression, the object of his attention was giving him some pleasure. Rue must have been aware of my presence for without shifting his gaze he lifted a finger to indicate silence and then beckoned me over. 'Cor,' he hissed. 'Take you a look at that!'

I took a look. The shed backed on to the garden of a neighbour, a man I don't know very well but who has some affluent job in the big city. Reposing on her stomach, all long, leggy and luscious in her birthday suit, was his Swedish au pair soaking up the sun. The garden was well screened so why not. 'I thought she'd be out there today,' whispered Ol' Rue. 'A beauty ain't she?'.

'I'm surprised at you Rue,' I said.

'Who are you to talk,' came his quick retort. 'Notice you took your time gettin' an eyeful!'

'I didn't mean it that way,' I protested, 'I meant I'm surprised at you looking at a wog.'

'A wog?' he said 'Don't be so daft, she ain't a wog, she's a gal. Gals ain't wogs.'

I'm still trying to puzzle that one out, and I've a good idea Ol' Rue's idol Unoch Powell would be equally perplexed.

Dealing with Darkie Birds

Any reader who thinks the above title heralds a titillating piece on amorous escapades with dusky maidens is going to be disappointed.

The darkie birds in question are rooks – the winged and wily creatures that delight in plundering my fields of sown grain. The seasonal battle of Me-versus-Them has long been a regular feature of this farming scene – and in this context there is no more apt and fitting word than scene.

My youthful introduction to their activities came as punishment for putting frog's jelly in the roadman's Wellington boots that stood unattended beside his barrow.

Unfortunately I did not see the roadman having his elevenses behind the hedge. Understandably irate, he took me by the scruff of my neck to face my father. 'If the boy ain't got nothing better to do than make himself a something nuisance,' he suggested, 'you'd best send him down your Sixteen Acre to deal with them darkie birds tha's peckin' your something corn to bits.'

At first this seemed a slight penalty to pay for an enterprise that, had it been successful, would have seen the roadman sink his foot into that lovely squelchy frog's jelly. But after a few days' banishment to the Sixteen Acre I began to feel otherwise.

Being an effective scarecrow became increasingly difficult. The rooks quickly evaluated the opposition and when disturbed would simply alight on another part of the field. Boredom and frustration were only saved by the end of the school holiday.

Since those days battle has been joined on many occasions, always in anger on my part.

Of course, at other than sowing times the darkie birds do not furrow the farmer's brow. One can see them most afternoons, high in the sky, like a great blitz of black bombers forging westward as if to keep up with the falling day. But wait until the grain is in the ground and then they come silently winging in over the tree tops to strike.

Just about every means and device in the book has been tried in an effort to combat their activities, but any success is temporary. The only salvation is that farmers all tend to sow grain around the same time, and thus it isn't always my fields that suffer the black horde. The worst thing is to sow when no one else does. Foolishly one winter I re-drilled patches in two fields where autumn germination was poor. It was a blunder of the highest magnitude. How the message got round to the rookery is a mystery, but the grain drill was no sooner back in the shed than Commander-in-Chief, East Suffolk Division, Rooks, was planning his campaign.

'That idiot over the hill has kindly provided us with winter sport, cor. A quarter acre in two fields half a mile apart, cor. Right, cor. We hit this field first, and if there's any trouble we move to the other, and so on, cor. Ready for take-off, right, cor, scramble!'

The attack was countered with the usual plastic bags on sticks, erratic bangers and other contrivances, all contemptuously ignored by the rooks. Occasionally, when passing near and catching sight of a host comfortably nourishing themselves, I would rush into the field waving my arms and uttering the most horrible noises. Very effective, but not durable – plus the risk that any unknowing observer may question one's sanity. Witness an occasion when, banging a piece of tin, gesticulating wildly and giving full voice to the most blood-curdling sounds, I suddenly became aware of the gentleman in a neighbouring garden staring in amazement. Unfortunately, by the time I had uttered an explanatory 'Rooks!' they had sloped off over the far hedge so there was nothing for him to see that might verify the purpose of this exhibition. I retreated sheepishly under his still incredulous gaze.

In view of the persistence of the attacks on these two plots, I resorted to a gun, knowing that if a rook could be slaughtered on the spot and its corpse displayed on a makeshift gibbet, its comrades would halt their visits. This was not easily achieved, for darkie birds appear to be able to distinguish between man harmless and man with a weapon. Even to stand a chance of success it is necessary to get down-wind, under cover and wait.

So, determined, I found myself a patch of dead vegetation near a footpath, laid down and waited. Eventually the plunderers started to arrive in ones and twos, gliding in over the trees. At the crucial moment, with my finger tightening on the trigger, I suddenly became aware of a panting sound, and to my chagrin a large French poodle hove in sight over my shoulder. Any dog worth its name would have barked, but not this creature. It began sniffing my person and wagging its sloppy tail. 'Go on!' I hissed, but, undeterred, it carried on with its nasal inspection. Then, to turn an irritating situation into an embarrassing one, a female voice called 'Jeremy, heel.' I raised an eye over the bent bracken and perceived a woman looking anxiously in my direction.

'You all right?' she enquired. 'After the darkie birds,' I replied, motioning with my head towards the open field – then realising too late that the rooks had disappeared, probably at the first appearance of the dog.

'Oh,' said the woman in a distinctly nervous tone, and went on her way, walking extremely briskly and twice glancing back at me. Although there was no longer any purpose – rookwise – in my continuing to lie in the bracken and dead nettles, I did not dare to get up until the woman was out of sight for fear that she might take to her heels, screaming. Consider the implications: a strange man dressed in baggy corduroy trousers and an old leather jerkin and wearing a red tea-cosy hat, hiding in weeds beside a foothpath and murmuring something about being after darkie birds – a term which obviously did not mean rooks to the woman; and she probably didn't see the gun either. Who would believe me?

So I've dropped that tactic and returned to the 'rushing into the field in anger' technique. Good exercise for the limbs and lungs if nothing else.

The Trouble
with Draughty Dodds

'Have a peppie,' said old Newson, offering a small crumpled paper bag containing a half dozen or so large white peppermints. 'Thanks,' I replied. 'I didn't realise they still made these; haven't seen any for years.'

He pressed one into his own mouth and rested himself comfortably against his garden gate. 'Nothing like 'em for settling the stomach, 'ticular if you've had too many spring greens for ya dinner. Not that I'm ever one to be troubled in that way. Still, a peppie is good for easin' the digestion; that'll put most people to rights.

'Course some's they won't – poor owd Draughty Dodds eat a couple of pound one day but they din't do him no good . . . You remember Draughty Dodds, don't yer?'

I didn't, but not wishing to be given a life history I mumbled 'Yes, I think I do . . .'

'Ah,' old Newson quickly rejoined, not to be thwarted. 'Course he was really afore your time; he must have bin 50 when you was a boy. Well, he was the toppin' fellow I ever did hear; his owd guts they played him up suffin' cruel. Like as if he had his own thunderstorm for ever a brewin' up inside; only trouble was now and again that would break out – both ends.

'It didn't help none his alus eatin' a whole raw onion with his bread and cheese come bait time and washing it down with home brewed beer – and that were a mite stronger than that duck-puddle

water that pass as ale down at the pub now let me tell yer.

'He was a great big fellow, stood a clear six foot, and he had a tidy pod on him too. Strong as a bullock and all the owd farmers liked him to work for 'em. I mind one sayin' how as Draughty was the best value he'd ever had in a man; good worker, kept the other men on their toes and had a built-in bird scarer as well.'

At this point there was an interlude for mirth in which I respectfully joined. After recovering his composure old Newson continued his unusual tale.

'As I was sayin' he was rare strong. Used to pump the church organ bellows of a Sunday – did it for years. Poor old Brown the organist was always complainin' there was somethin' wrong with the organ. He never did discover where all those extra bass notes was comin' from!

'Draughty volunteered for the army in the war – that's the

Kaiser's. But they wouldn't have him. An officer wrote on his papers, "This man is apparently already engaged in hostilities. If he can first bring his own private conflict to a conclusion then we can use him." 'Course they had him in the Home Guard durin' the last lot. Use' to liven up the parades I can tell yer.

'Never married – well what woman would put up with lying with the likes of him all night? Never get a mite of sleep. 'Sides, I alus wonder how he kept the sheets on his bed unless they was tied down. 'Course he got worse as the years went by, but didn't worry Draughty. He alus thought it was a great joke.'

'What happened to him?' I enquired (on reflection, foolishly).

'Well, you mind the time little owd Hitler was sending over them Doodly Bugs?'

'Doodle Bugs,' I corrected.

'Thas right, Doodly Bugs,' he persisted. 'One night one of them lands right on poor old Draughty's cottage – well, thas what they said.'

He leaned forward over the gate and continued in a confidential tone. 'But how come they didn't find no bits of Doodly Bug? No, if you ask me owd Draughty was took with an almighty collision of wind and water and up he goes like one of them 'tomic bombs. Stands t' reason somethin' like that would happen one day.'

It was probably my look of incredulous disbelief that old Newson misinterpreted and led to his next remark: 'You're lookin' a bit queezy. Here, have another peppie, that'll soon put you to rights.'

I took a handful!

Wernie

There was a time when everyone on the farm referred to the police as the 'po-lice'. It is quite common for certain words to be deliberately given distorted pronunciation by a family or group of associates, the reason usually being no deeper than an intangible pleasure in abusing the Queen's English. In the case of 'po-lice', however, this stemmed from attempts by a German ex-prisoner of war who once worked on the farm to master a foreign tongue. When first released from prison camp he was required to report to our local bobby at regular intervals. 'I haf go zee das po-lice,' he would proclaim. The poor fellow was undoubtedly mystified by our amusement, but at that stage in his understanding of English it would have been useless to explain what a 'po' was, or, for that matter, 'lice'. Nevertheless, for many, many years the constabulary were known as the po-lice – behind their backs of course. Sadly, no more, as I must be the only one left on the farm who remembers Wernie.

I can see him now, British battle dress dyed brown with a large white disc sewn on the back of the jacket; Wermacht field cap also dyed brown; and underneath its peak a young, rounded, beaming face, not at all what one would have expected of a vanquished enemy. His tall, upright stature contrasted sharply with that of our shortish and stooped workforce.

The Guv'nor had informed us that he was taking on an ex-Jerry prisoner to help with the harvest and perhaps permanently. He

46

hoped we would treat the man as an equal and maybe he would learn a few things about democracy. Well, I don't know about democracy; but he certainly learned a few things.

Despite his protestations that his name was pronounced 'Verner', all of us continued with the anglicised version. As Wully put it bluntly: 'If he's bin spelt with a W so he'll be said with a W.' Inevitably the strange English habit of changing perfectly presentable names by terminating them with 'ie' was applied to Werner and thus our German farmhand quickly became Wernie to all and sundry.

Wernie's command of English was, at first, very limited and we sometimes hadn't the foggiest idea what he was on about, even when his flow of words was accompainied by much gesticulation. On his first day with us, when despatched to help drive some bullocks to pasture, he gave a whelp of delight and ran to embrace the oak in the bottom meadow. The British are accustomed to eccentrics but I know we other bullock drivers were quite taken aback by this display. Aware of our astonishment, Wernie, arms still spread around the trunk, volunteered a sort of explanation: 'Zis is  gooed. Zis is das ock.' Not that we were really any the wiser. After a minute or so of murmuring in German to the tree he disengaged himself and came grinning back to us.

Wully, who had beheld all this, commented in his usual obscene and cryptic way, questioning Wernie's sanity. Then, as an afterthought, he added: 'Well, I s'pose flingin' his arms round a tree 'll do him less harm than if it was a woman.'

Next day we had a repeat performance, this time with the old oak at the top of Ten Acre. As soon as Wernie clapped eyes on it, off he sped to embrace it. 'Zis is das ock. Zis is very gooed.' In fact, during the following weeks Wernie must have hugged every oak on the farm! There was much speculation on this curious performance. Most put it down to over-exuberance at his new-found freedom, although the Guv'nor's wife thought Wernie might belong to some religious cult of forest worshippers. Wully, as might be expected, made crude suggestions about Germans making love to trees. The truth, eventually extracted when Wernie's English improved, was much more understandable. Prior to his capture in France his column of troops had been bombed. One bomb had exploded only a few yards from Wernie, who was saved by the bulk of an oak trunk behind which he had taken shelter. Thus he felt indebted to this redoubtable species and eager to express his gratitude.

Everybody came to accept and like Wernie, even Wully who had been 'shot at by them Jerry buggers' in the First World War. Wernie was hard working, bright and usually cheerful. The only time I can recall him being a bit morose was when asked why he chose to stay in England and not return to his native land. On this point he would shrug his shoulders and half sigh. 'It is no good there any more. Better here.'

Wernie was quick to pick up most things, but he did have trouble with our language, the more so because of local dialect. However, the Guv'nor's wife appreciated the situation and patiently encouraged his widening vocabulary, not without some unfortunate hiccups. She had an aged motor lawnmower which needed extraordinary patience and considerable stamina to start. She was always trotting out into the yard to find one of us to perform the job. If forewarned of her intention to mow the lawn those of us who had struggled with the brute before tried to absent ourselves from the farmyard. The helpful Wernie, unaware of the reputation of this dreadful machine, was quick to volunteer. The experience must have been a shock because afterwards I heard him plaintively enquiring why it was so difficult to start – if his words weren't clear, his meaning was obvious – and receiving the sort of useless reply you would expect from Wully. It was Wernie who fell foul of the Guv'nor's wife next time the lawn had to be mowed. As Wernie sweated over the pull start, the Guv'nor's wife soothingly observed that she wondered why the machine was always so difficult to bring to life. Wernie brightened, for he could provide the solution: 'It is all fokkered up!' he announced triumphantly. The Guv'nor's wife kept her composure, even when he requested: 'You get engine man mend fokkered up?' The Guv'nor's wife guessed the origin of this advice and chose to ignore it in the hope Wernie would soon come to have a better appreciation of the vagaries of our language. Alas, more direct action proved necessary, for a few days later, while discussing her garden with Wernie, the Guv'nor's wife mentioned the boy who helped on Saturday mornings and received the enthusiastic comment: 'Ya, Wully zay his lazy fokker.' Again she kept her composure but later burned the Guv'nor's ear with demands that something be done about foul language on the farm and that Wernie be advised that he should not repeat all he heard verbatim.

Next day the Guv'nor took Wernie aside and with some embarrassment and much difficulty explained there were certain 'bad words' that one should be careful not to use. Eventually Wernie caught on. The only trouble being that thereafter he suspected every new adjective encountered as 'ze bad word', and as you can guess, people had a joke at his expense by persuading him that perfectly innocent words were taboo. In desperation Wernie requested I write down all 'ze bad words' for him, an unusual task in which, I regret to admit, I took great delight.

Unfortunately, this had a result I had not anticipated, for Wernie, anxious to impress that he would err no more, showed the Guv'nor the list. The Guv'nor was somewhat taken aback by his son's knowledge of invective, obscenities and verbal filth, so much so that he later remarked to a neighbouring farmer that the list contained much that was new to him. For me, however, he had sharp words, accusing me of peddling filth to Wernie and saying that I should set an example to others, not drag them into the gutter. Nevertheless, while I was in disgrace at home, Wernie thought highly of my efforts.

One day it occurred to me that there could be satisfaction in being able to parrot a few German 'bad vords'. When, for example, the Guv'nor gave me a task I did not like I would be able to

curse him out loud without his being aware of it. With persever-
ance I was able to persuade Wernie to divulge a number of German
'bad vords' and thereafter use them with vigour on appropriate
occasions. Wernie, however, must have suspected my purpose,
for years later a German friend was much amused to inform me
that my supposed curses were mild compliments. Wernie's version of the German for 'You can stick your —— up your ——'
turned out to be 'Your breath is like a thousand roses.'

Eventually Wernie's command of English improved to a point
where he was able to ask a local war widow to marry him. This and
her acceptance were probably not dependent upon language, for,
from my observations in a nearby wood, biological chemistry had
a lot to do with it. Anyway, they married and moved from the
district, Wernie's ambitions to better himself being put to the test.
Indeed, his enterprise brought prosperity and from the village
stores that he and his wife acquired there sprang a chain of grocery
shops in several West Country towns. The last I heard of Wernie
was that he had sold out to a supermarket consortium for two
million pounds and retired to a Georgian mansion set in 25 acres of
parkland. His wealth was well earned and deserved, but I can't help
wondering if that parkland is full of oaks.

That Which is Lost is . . .

One would have had a job to find a harder working and more conscientious fellow than Archie. There was no stopping him when there were crops to plant or harvest, his tractor was out of the shed long before the Guv'nor had opened an eyelid on the new day, and its headlights would just as surely be splashing across the furrows when the 'malt and hops brigade' were ushered burping out of the local pub at 10.35 p.m. The fruits of his labours could be seen in the form of a bright new car and the purchase of his own house.

Archie was almost the perfect farm operative – almost. His one weakness could be termed a lack of mechanical aptitude; or perhaps he was just unlucky where machines were concerned; and then again there is the blunt view expressed by village folk who envied him his new car that Archie was 'only fit to drive a sledge-hammer'.

However you like to describe it, one thing is certain. Machines did tend to come to bits when being used by Archie. Invariably this occurred in the fields when he was usually so busy trying to finish the job that he didn't see the pieces go. An awful lot of bits were lost in the soil and for variety he managed to add the odd spanner and a personal item or two. Such was the regularity of reported loss that I decided to keep an inventory during the six years up to Archie's retirement. It includes 31 plough shares, two plough discs, two cultivator tines, 14 spring tines, one seed harrow, an oil can, numerous hand tools, a Thermos flask, a packet of Fox's Glacier Mints, four pen-knives and 79 pence in small change. Odd pieces of machines in profusion made up the bulk of this list and such was and is the wealth of metal in our fields that I have seriously considered buying a metal detector.

Of course, as we sow we reap. Regularly the earth reveals some rust-encrusted relic of bygone days – alas, usually too bygone, and stemming from an implement long since disposed of. One twisted piece of iron caught up in a harrow was identified by Archie as 'a dinger off an owd pummle hoe.'

'So it is,' I said knowledgeably, not wishing to admit that I hadn't the faintest idea what a pummle hoe was, let alone a dinger.

The way those that were lost were and are found can be disastrous. One autumn I was hobbling over a field where Archie was bounding to and fro over the clods with tractor and power harrow. My purpose was to encourage him to progress a little more steadily, but before I could attract his attention there was a violent crash, bang, wallop, wallop, thump, thump, tinkle, tinkle, clomp and tractor and power harrow came to an abrupt halt in a cloud of dust. Archie and I eyed each other, long faced, but for me vision was mentally blurred by escaping pound signs. The last time the power harrow had done a minor crash, bang, and wallop it cost us more for repair parts than the machine was worth. As I staggered the few remaining yards towards the scene of the disaster I could hear the chairman of the manufacturers reporting another good year.

Reality returned and I became conscious of Archie standing by the power harrow, holding something up, and shouting cheerful words my way. 'Thought we'd find this one day. We lost it when you was still at school. Always reckoned it got left on the bottom of a cart and tipped off with a load of muck. Good strong chain – thas about 18 foot long.'

As Archie had hold of only about seven feet of chain, the rest was obviously wrapped round the machine's rotors. It was, and took precisely two hours and seven minutes of time, an incredible amount of banging, prying and pulling, several bits of severed skin and a helping of best-quality invective to free the thing. However, to my amazement the crash, bang, and wallop miraculously resulted in no breakages and the power harrow could continue merrily on its way.

So we did gain a very strong, useful chain. I say did, because a few weeks later we were looking for it and couldn't find it. Archie said he had it down in the wood to haul a dead tree out of the way, but he was sure he brought it back. But then he said he also had it to wrap round the drawbar of a broken disc harrow – but again he was sure he put the chain back in the shed.

All this gave me an uncomfortable feeling that one day – not necessarily that year or the next – but one day, someone is going to be tripping over the fields with a machine when there is going to be an almighty great 'crash, bang, wallop, wallop, thump, thump, tinkle, tinkle, clomp' – and heaven help us! It hasn't happened yet, but it will.

An Unholly Situation

There is something cheery and seasonal about a holly bush bright with berries. Yet I have known Christmases when none of the holly trees and bushes around here showed a single spot of red. At other times, while many hollies are completely bare, a few will be loaded with berries.

The explanation for this is obscure unless one believes that once proffered by old Newson, with all the wisdom of his 80 years.

'The reason yer get berries on some bushes and none on others is that some hollies are male and some's female. That grut old bush top on your sixteen acre, thas a male, that never have nothin' on it. But that little one down the hedge by the brook is a gal, 'cause it ain't often thas without berries. Stands to reason that them two mate.'

'Mate?' I said incredulously.

'Yes, o' course they do, I jus' told yer there's male and female. O' course yer do get 'mophridite hollies and they mates themselves. What's more holly only mates at night. Them variagated ones with no prickles is always females and they mate best. Don't often see them with no berries.'

The thought of great prickly male bushes uprooting themselves after dark and rushing round the countryside in search of a defenceless variegated maid in somebody's shrubbery was too much and I could not contain my mirth.

Old Newson shut his right eye and gave me a scornful look. 'Ah, don't be a darn fool, you knows hollies mates by wind, same as other trees. If we don't have draughty nights in the summer then we don't get no berries on the holly. You got to have wind at night to carry the pollen.'

I recall one Christmas before I had reached my majority, when there was almost a complete absence of berried holly. I searched every bush on the farm for a sprig but all in vain. The only berries to be seen that year were on a beautiful variegated tree that stood in the front garden of a local house. This splendid specimen had been well tended over the years, the lower shoots having been trimmed off so that six feet of trunk supported a dense mass of foliage in a classic shape. The house, home of a widow, Mrs Marsfield, had at some time been renamed 'The Hollies' in honour of the tree.

At the time of this dearth of holly berries we had on the farm a worker called Nasty. He was known to everyone as Nasty and rather seemed to delight in this uncomplimentary nickname. In truth I cannot now remember what his real name was. He must then have been about 20 years older than me, in his late thirties, and physically rather attractive, with thick curly hair and a fine-boned face.

Nasty was not altogether popular with his workmates – although he never worked anywhere long enough to have many – because of his rather high opinion of himself and his prowess. 'Bumptious' was the word for Nasty. He also had the habit of finding things before they were lost, which resulted in the odd skirmish with the local law.

One morning when Nasty arrived for work he hailed me: 'Boy, do yer know where there's any holly? I've promised her at the Anchor a bunch.' I explained that I had been unable to find any on the farm and the only berried tree around was that in Mrs Marsfield's garden.

Nasty had probably been promised a couple of pints by the landlady at the Anchor, because he was intent on getting hold of some holly by fair means or foul – and it was to be foul.

'Tell yer what, boy, come five o'clock and we'll pop up the road and nip a bit of Ma Marsfield's. Part of that ol' tree hang over the road anyway, so it'll be public property.'

I wasn't convinced of any right to help ourselves, but somehow I got talked into assisting in this venture. After work I met Nasty in the cart lodge, where he produced a pair of pruning shears and a sack. Evidently he wanted more than a bunch – he was probably taking orders in the pub at lunchtime.

We set off in the darkness towards our objective, which was situated in a fairly isolated position near the top of the hill leading to the village. Leaving our cycles in the field beside Mrs Marsfield's garden we climbed the fence into her shrubbery.

'How much do yer want?' enquired Nasty.

'Oh, only a small bunch,' I quailed, courage flagging.

'Now this is what we'll do,' continued Nasty. 'I'll go across the lawn and shin up the tree. You go out on the road and pick up the pieces as I snip 'em off. If a car or anybody comes along you nip back in the shrubbery until they're past. No one will see me with the tree being so thick. I'll just sit tight.'

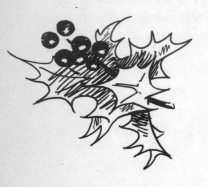

The holly stood in a large lawn without any bushes around it to conceal Nasty's form as he crept across and shinned up the tree. As he drew himself up into the foliage a twig cracked and a host of small birds, disturbed from their roost, went fluttering away into the night. None of the windows in the front of the house were lit, suggesting that the widow was in her back kitchen and oblivious of the tell-tale sounds of the assault being mounted on her property. A faint snip followed by a slight rustling and the first sprig came floating down on the roadside path. While retrieving this I heard distant voices. 'Somebody's coming up the hill,' I hissed and ran back into the shrubbery. Presently two shapes, one large, one small, appeared through the gloom; they could only be Maisie and Percy pushing their cycles home from work at the village grocer's.

A courtship had blossomed between these two and, having flourished for six or seven years, the gossips were intrigued as to when – if ever – the knot would be tied. Moreover, these two were, behind their backs, the butt of many a joke, Maisie being all of 18 stone, a really colossal woman, whereas Percy was a small man, lean and about eight inches shorter than his lady friend. The prospect of this alliance was a favourite subject for the more unsavoury elements frequenting the taproom of the Anchor. 'He's a doomed man if he marry her,' was one comment. 'If she turn over in her sleep she'll suffocate the poor little perisher.' Most of the other speculations about the physical problems of the proposed union were unprintable.

The road was level enough at The Hollies for Maisie and Percy to remount their cycles and presently I heard the protesting creaks of Maisie's machine as she settled her weight on the saddle. The two shapes accelerated past the tree where Nasty was concealed, but a few yards further and there was a stifled cry as the larger of the two shapes came to an abrupt halt.

There followed alarmed enquiries from Percy, answered with stifled moans and grunts from an obviously winded Maisie. It transpired that the end of her long woollen muffler had caught in the front wheel of the cycle and wound up like a reel, so that Maisie was almost kissing the tyre. Percy was frantically trying to unravel the situation when a car swung round the corner, illuminating the scene as it passed. Maisie jack-knifed over the handlebars and Percy crouched over the front wheel, head towards hers. There was a screech of brakes and the car came to a halt a little way down the hill, but, after a second or two the driver moved on again – probably thinking he had witnessed some strange courting rite enacted in these parts.

Nasty could well have dislodged himself from the tree and stolen away unnoticed during all this commotion, but when Percy banged on Mrs Marsfield's front door for help and that lady switched on her porch light, partly illuminating the area around the tree, the opportunity for undetected escape was gone.

Mrs Marsfield produced a torch to help Percy free his crumpled love, afterwards inviting the shocked and pained Maisie into the house to recuperate.

In his concern for Maisie, Percy had forgotten to remove her cycle from where it lay in the road. As soon as I heard a vehicle approaching I anticipated what would happen, but was frozen into immobility by guilt. Although the local fish-and-chip man always drove his van like a maniac – presumably to get away from the smell that was always trailing him – it can be said in his favour that on this occasion he was quick to apply the brakes the moment Maisie's cycle was exposed by his headlights.

But, alas, he was not quick enough. There was a clattering din as the van struck the cycle, then a roar from the engine as the exhaust silencer was torn off. On the other hand, the van came to a halt too quickly for some of the contents of the vehicle, which cascaded sizzling through the serving hatch.

The fish-and-chip man remonstrated with Percy and Percy remonstrated with the fish-and-chip man, and now and then Mrs Marsfield chipped in with her say. They were trying to pull pieces of the cycle out from under the van when, to my horror, the familiar form of our local policeman appeared, treading carefully between the soggy chips and rock salmon. My courage failed completely. Besides, it was well past teatime and my mother got very upset if anyone was late. It began to rain as I crept out of the shrubbery into the meadow, and by the time I got home it was pouring down. The rain did not let up for at least an hour, after which my curiosity as to whether Nasty had been apprehended or not got the better of my nervousness.

Nasty's cycle was still in the field, the policeman was sipping tea in Mrs Marsfield's porch and the local garage men were busy with a hacksaw trying to liberate a piece of cycle which was entwined round the prop-shaft of the van. Nothing moved in the holly tree but Nasty must still have been there. At least it wasn't a prickly perch.

Nasty didn't show up for work next day and later my father received word that he was in bed with a touch of pneumonia. 'Been on the beer again more than likely', was my father's observation. Knowing the truth, I was more concerned, although it was probably fear of ridicule that kept Nasty away; he was seen in the pub the following night, as chirpy as ever, helping the brewers' profits – at somebody else's expense no doubt.

On Christmas Eve I sighted the local bobby cycling nonchalantly out of Mrs Marsfield's with a large bunch of holly, thereby providing a moral to this tale – although I doubt if Nasty would ever have seen it.

Somebody's
Pinched Me Puddin'

This is partly an admission of weakness and partly a warning; or, come to think of it, an advertisement for British cottage industry – to put it nicely.

It happened when I went to look at an emerging cereal crop. While pondering the possibility that the field just inspected was not wheat with a few wild oats but wild oats with a few spears of wheat, a familiar voice hailed me from across the road.

'Afternoon, young master.'

I assume he considered this address to be flattering but, since I thought myself neither young nor masterly, I found it simply ridiculous.

'Afternoon, Mr Newson.'

'Been keepin' an eye out for you,' he called. 'Do you come here and try some of my brew.' He was poised in his cottage doorway, through which flames licking logs in a grate highlighted his form in a rather satanical if cheering way. 'Well,' I replied, trying desperately to think of some excuse, 'I really . . .'

'You ain't agoin' to tell me you're in a hurry. I bin watchin' you wanderin' about in that field this last quarter hour – jus' like an owd dog was tryin' to pick up the scent of a bone it's buried. 'Sides, you got to get used to a spot of good wine. You'll be drinkin' it mornin', noon and night when that Common Market takes us over completely. Jus' like them Frogs.'

There followed a monologue on French habits with wine, based on old Newson's experiences in '18 and which would undoubtedly give Mary Whitehouse concern. For want of an excuse I could only accept old Newson's hospitality, although well aware that once in his parlour it was a job to get away. He does tend to run on a bit.

'Now this is me sloe,' he said, uncorking an old vinegar bottle and pouring a fair amount of the contents into a large tumbler.

'Steady,' I said. 'I don't drink much you know.'

'Gawd boy, this 'ont hurt you. Give you courage. Why I mind my nephew over at Hadleigh – he was a nervous boy he was – hadn't the courage to go courtin' unless he'd had a swig of sloe.'

'Did it do any good?' I asked.

'Must 'a done. He's got 12 kids now,' he rejoined, without a hint of humour.

'This is very nice,' I said, sampling the sloe.

'Well, empty your glass and we'll see what you think of me dandelion,' he countered. My polite protests were swept aside and from a cupboard he produced another bottle, dusted it with the hem of his jacket and proceeded to fill a small whisky glass. 'Won't give you much 'cause my daughter is partial to this and I must save a drop for her – she's bringin' her two boys over this afternoon.' Somewhat relieved at not having to do justice to a half tumbler full, I drank his health with relish. It was a most pleasing wine to my palate. 'There's not many what know how to make dandelion proper nowadays,' old Newson confided, lowering his voice and leaning across the table as if he were about to impart a vital secret. 'You has to pick 'em before the sun is up and starts drawin' the sap. 'Course, there's some what say you should pick 'em while the dew's still on 'em but I don't go that far. Never know whether thas dew or if some owd cow been lickin' round 'em would you?' Suddenly the dandelion didn't seem quite so tasty.

Old Newson returned to his cupboard and retrieved a large stone jar. What apprehension I could muster bade me be off, but my resistance was obviously low. Another large tumbler was put on the table. It was opaque with age and the glass must have been a quarter of an inch thick. The liquid that flowed from the stone jar was also opaque. I managed to say 'Steady on!' as the level rose, but he had firmly decided the measure of his generosity. 'Now', proclaimed my host, 'this is me mushroom!'

'Your what?'

'Me mushroom,' he repeated with a note of triumph.

'I didn't know you could make mushroom wine,' I said.

'Not many can; but thas more a spirit than a wine – do you try it.'

'It is a bit strong,' I said, sipping cautiously.

'First you mus' be sure you've got mushrooms. There was a rare to-do some years ago when owd Mrs Markwhite made some out of toadstools by mistake. She took a bottle along to the Mothers Meeting for all the owd dears to try. 'Course, that near poisoned 'em. Doctor had to use his stirrup pump on 'em.'

'Stomach pump,' I corrected.

'Yes, he had to stirrup pump half the owd gals in the village,' he persisted.

'I got the recipe time I was living down Maldon way. There were an owd widow lived in the village that used to make all manner of wine and stuff and I got it from her. She was a dab hand at wine and no one could touch her when it came to Christmas puddin'. Folk would come for miles to get her to make a Christmas puddin' for them, they were that good. I mind there was a gent came all the way from Ipswich to get one of her puddins every year – until he got into trouble. You see, one Christmas when he went to get his puddin' she gave him a bottle of this 'ere mushroom. What she didn't know was that this owd gent was a bit weak over drink. I alus reckoned he weren't quite the ticket. They say when he was a lad he fell out of a tree and landed astride a holly bush. Never the same after that.'

'Ouch!' I winced.

'Here, have a little more,' said old Newson, again pouring from the stone jar. I wanted to protest, but my attention was diverted by having to hold down the table, which kept trying to rise and tilt.

'Well,' he continued, warming to his tale, 'this owd boy kept stoppin' his car on the way home and havin' a little tipple of mushroom. Folk don't know exactly what happened but come two o'clock in the mornin' a constable found him sittin' on the steps of Ipswich Town Hall yellin' at the top of his voice: "Somebody's pinched me puddin'." Fact, the owd East Anglian Daily Times had a headline next day saying "Who Stole Who's Puddin'." '

I never did hear the rest of the story – not that I cared at the time – as just then the bus stopped outside the house. 'Well, here's me daughter,' said old Newson. 'I'd best put the kettle on.' I remember making my escape and en route to the gate tripping over something on the path, only to discover I wasn't walking up the path but the middle of Newson's herbaceous border. At this point I passed his daughter who was looking rather amazed. I intended to say good afternoon but, curiously, what came out was 'Somebody's pinched me puddin'.' She gave me one of those freezing looks only women can give, but it did not have the sobering effect it should have done. Not until I had spent some minutes trying to unlatch Newson's garden gate at the hinge end did an appreciation of the full potency of 'the mushroom' begin to dawn on me. And after that I can't really remember much at all – apart from the thick head that lingered for days.

The Christmas Box

I have always had a very soft spot for the old countrymen of my youth – those generations that had their own childhood before aeroplanes, motor cars, electricity and radio were known in rural parts. They were mostly grand old men, charitable to others, but though times were hard they never sought charity for themselves. At Christmas they entered into the spirit of things with fervour, and if their gifts – always called Christmas boxes – were simple by today's standards, they were always given with sincerity and received with gratitude.

If old fellows had money to spend, then a small boy would receive a 'hapeth' of sweets, but more often the gift would be something that had cost time rather than money such as a pop-gun fashioned from an elder stub. Their presents for one another were also usually of their own creation, and many a potent bottle of elderberry or cowslip wine would change hands.

In this village there were two lovable old codgers who brought an original twist to the custom of exchanging Christmas boxes. The object was to give one another something ridiculous that cost nothing but would cause a great deal of merriment. I do not know when this custom began, but both men had worked on the same farm for a great many years and the annual exchange had become something of a ritual. On the morning of Christmas Eve they would arrive early for work, present each other with an outlandish gift, and then drown their mirth with a pint of home-made beer –

this alone being guaranteed to put them in a good mood for the rest of the day. As both men have children and grandchildren still living in this neighbourhood I will call them by the fictitious names of Bill and Bob.

In the early days the contents of the brown-paper parcels exchanged could be such things as a piece of mouldy cheese or a boot with no sole, a spoon with a hole in it, a rotten egg, and so on. On only one occasion, so I am told, was there ever an exchange of identical gifts and this was due to some joker sowing the idea separately to both Bill and Bob. Both parcels contained sparrows drawn and trussed ready for the oven. Both Bill and Bob had sizeable paunches in their waning years and the great hilarity of those festive occasions can truly be said to have been belly laughter. As the years passed the contents of the Christmas parcels tended to become more and more revolting as each man sought to outdo the other.

It got to the stage where the revolting was fast becoming the outrageously disgusting to less earthy souls.

Fate, however, stepped in to caution them. One icy Christmas Eve in the late Thirties, Bill was negotiating a corner on the way to work when his cycle went into a nasty skid, and but for a nifty piece of recovery action, the corpulent Bill, cycle and all, would have been splattered across the road. As it was, part of the 'all' did topple out of Bill's carrier box, though unobserved by the rather nerve-shaken rider. Not until he arrived in the farmyard did Bill discover that his gift for Bob was missing from the carrier box.

Greatly concerned, Bill hastily pedalled back to the scene of the skid, but there was no sign of the large brown-paper parcel – only the roadman who had arrived and was sanding the slippery surface. Normally Bill would have been quick to pass a few choice remarks about roadmen who didn't get out early enough in the morning, but it was the roadman who opened the conversation. 'You lookin' for somethin'?' he said.

'I thought something might have dropped out of my box when I come along here just now,' replied Bill, sheepishly.

'There were,' said the roadman. 'When I came along a great brown-paper parcel lay on the side of the road but before I was anywhere near it old Miss Thingamy come runnin' out of her house and took it back indoors. You best go and see her.' Even more sheepishly Bill mumbled, 'No I ain't lost nothing like that,' and cycled off.

To this day people around here still speculate on the ghastly contents of that parcel, for Bill never said a word. Neither did Miss Thingamy – no that wasn't her real name, of course – who, apart from being renowned for an extremely inquisitive nature, obviously had no other course but to open an unlabelled parcel to see if there was any clue to the sender's identity. For a while this incident tempered the enthusiasm of Bill and Bob to surpass each other, but the Christmas Eve custom still went on even after both were retired.

They have all gone now – Miss Thingamy in 1939. Some said she never got over the shock. Bill passed away in 1948 and Bob six years later.

When Bob was getting hard of breath and they sent for the Chapel minister, it is said that he asked the good man: 'I ain't ever bin one for much chapel goin' but I'd take it kindly Reverend if you could put in a good word for me so as I goes to the same place as Bill Whatsit. He'll need an old mate around cause he's bound to be a bit embarrassed if that Miss Thingamy's there too.'

It seems that Bob's request was met, because a fellow who works on that farm nowadays vowed he heard ghostly laughter at about 7.00 a.m. last Christmas Eve. Mind you, this fellow had been propping up the bar at the Anchor for a couple of hours when he made this startling revelation. Even so, it's nice to think of old Bill and old Bob still at it up there – but if they are, then that place has certainly become a lot more permissive.

The Snowbolt

The older you get the more you find that places and situations trigger memories, not necessarily nostalgic and often of trivial significance. Why, for instance, when I drive by the field at Black Brook Hill, which we gave up farming 40 years ago, do I recall bumping up and down in a tumbrel going in the gate. Lots of far more interesting or entertaining memories associated with that field can be retrieved, so why is that particular one the first to spring to mind? Puzzling. On the other hand, a persistent recollection that hits me whenever I venture onto the Hilly Field in snowy weather is undoubtedly associated with a particular spectacle.

It was a January day in the mid-Seventies. There had been a fair sprinkling of snow overnight and more was forecast. Old Rue, true to form, had come into work and informed me he was going to carry on with a bit of brushing and hedging he had started over on the far side of the Hilly. Mentioning the forecast of heavy snow, I suggested he might prefer to keep warm mucking out a calf box. No, he said, there wouldn't be much snow and not enough to stop his hedging activities. This was typical of Rue, cantankerous old so-and-so. Being retired and only doing part-time work of his choosing, there was no need for him to have left the warmth of his fireside on a day like that.

Around eleven o'clock it started to snow hard. As there was no let-up after half an hour, I became a little concerned about our 75-year-old pensioner and set off to see where he had got to.

69

Reaching the bottom of the Hilly Field, I looked up from under my umbrella and beheld an extraordinary sight. The snow was falling so heavily that it was impossible to tell where the brow of the hill met the sky: heaven and earth were one vast white void. And there, plumb in the centre, was the black smudge of Ol' Rue making his way back down the hill, yet appearing as if he was suspended in the whiteness. A strange spectacle, and easy to understand why it comes so readily to mind in snowy weather.

One might say Ol' Rue had an affinity with snow. When he was a young man he walked onto a snow covered pond by mistake and was submerged up to his shoulders in water when the ice under the snow gave way. In the very hard winter of . . . 1921, I think he said, when Ol' Rue lived in a cottage over near Westleton, he was snowed in for ten days and the family nearly ran out of food. Then there is his oft-told story of courting a girl in the snow, which does

not bear repeating here. And above all, of course, his encounter with a snowbolt, an experience he recalls every winter as soon as the first crystal flakes flutter down to earth. What is a snowbolt? You may well ask, for it does not appear in any dictionary. It is, in fact, wholly an invention of Ol' Rue's as far as I am aware. Let me tell you the story surrounding an event which, by chance, I happened to witness.

The time was February 1956, of that I am sure. There had been a prolonged cold spell, not a lot of snow but persistent hard frosts. On this particular day a gale of some strength had sprung up from the east, drifting the little snow on the fields so that most were fairly bare and their surfaces hard frozen. It was a bitterly cold day. Ol' Rue had elected to brush out a ditch on the far boundary of the farm. The Guv'nor had suggested jobs in the sheds but, true to his obstinate way, Rue insisted that the weather was no obstacle to him carrying on with the brushing he had begun the previous morning. Even in those days, when Rue was still in full-time work – he was then around 57 or 58 – he was more or less allowed to pick his own jobs on the farm. This came about through his self-appointment as unofficial foreman, ushering others into tackling the important jobs while leading the way. At morning start I often heard him say to the Guv'nor things like: 'I'll be takin' them (the other employees) down to the Eleven Acre. You'll be wantin' to start liftin' those mangels now its dry.' Or, 'We'll be off to turn that hay so thas ready when the sun break out' and other such suggestions that pre-empted the Guv'nor's orders. Rue had been around so long he could almost read the Guv'nor's mind. If there was no vital task at hand then he would be off on some maintenance job of his own choosing. The only on-the-farm company he really seemed to enjoy was his own.

It so happened that on this particular icy day I had been given time off to go shopping in town with my fiancee, wedding bells being scheduled for the end of the week. As we drove home that afternoon the gale was at its peak, so strong the gusts seemed they might sweep my little Austin straight off the road. Coming along the lane dividing the high land on our farm from that of the neighbour's prairie, my future wife and I were treated to an amazing sight. Our neighbour, who even in the Fifties was way ahead of most in the district with new techniques and innovations, had a cluster of large grain-storage bins beside his buildings. These bins were simply curved galvanised-steel sheets bolted together to extend to about 15 feet in height and 12 feet in diameter. They stood on a concrete apron and each was capped with a hefty lid made of wooden planks covered with roofing felt. Normally the weight of the lid would hold the galvanised cylinder in place. Unfortunately our neighbour had not allowed for such a forceful wind and, as we approached, the wooden lid on one silo half flipped and fell off. Almost immediately the empty silo blew over, there evidently being nothing to secure it around the base. Then, gradually picking up speed, it began to roll before the wind.

I brought the car to a stop, as it appeared the silo was going to bowl out across the road and come to rest in the ditch. It certainly rolled across the road, but it went right over the top of the roadside ditch. Ahead lay a ten acre field belonging to our neighbour and beyond that one of ours of similar size that curved away down to the valley. Then I caught sight of a familiar figure in the boundary ditch between the two – Rue, bent over, slashing away at the bank. The cylinder of steel sheet was rolling straight in his direction. The power of the wind was surprising – the silo was now moving at the speed of a running man. Like a shot I was out of the car, waving and shouting, but all in vain – the noise of the gale drowned my voice. Still the silo rolled on and still Rue continued his work, oblivious of what was bearing down on him. All I could do was watch in horror and pray that Rue would look up. Just before the silo reached the far side of the field I saw Rue raise his head and immediately drop out of sight as the thing thundered right over the top of him. Such was the momentum of the silo that it was not arrested by the stumpy hedge but smashed through and rolled on. No head emerged from the ditch. Fearing the worst, I jumped the roadside ditch and set off towards where I had last seen Rue. I hadn't covered many yards before, much to my relief, I saw him. He climbed up onto the bank, looking in the direction where the silo had disappeared from view over the brow of the hill and down into the valley. As he seemed none the worse for what must have been a nasty fright, I was not going to struggle across the field, and so returned to the car.

Later that day I learned that the wayward silo had finally come to rest some three quarters of a mile away from its home base after smashing into Comey Smith's chicken house and partly disintegrating. Mrs Smith was so terrified that she locked the doors and crawled under the bed, believing an aeroplane had crashed. Comey Smith, who never missed a trick, came out of it very well, having had a 50 per cent increase in hen numbers as soon as he heard of our neighbour's insurance. The more so considering he sold off the casualties quickly and half the village was eating chicken for the next two weeks.

I did not see Rue again until the following morning, by then assuming he had told everyone else on the farm about his narrow squeak. No sooner had I appeared in the farmyard than he hailed me with: 'You missed something yesterday when you was in town. A snowbolt.'

'What's a snowbolt?' I countered.

'Surely you knows what a snowbolt is? You's heard of a thunderbolt? Well, they's like that only made of snow. You get 'em when there's a gale what whip the snow up into a big ball and speed that along, getting bigger all the time.'

'First I've heard of such a thing,' I replied in disbelieving tone.

'Well you should have been here yesterday, you'd have seen one. Bloody near got me. I was in the ditch at Top Field a brushin' when I hears this roar like thunder. Just has time to see it comin' straight at me, big as a cart shed, must abin doin' 20 mile an hour. I had to fall flat on me back to miss it and bloody near got sufficated with snow. Really thought I was a goner.'

He firmly rejected my suggestion of his snowbolt being a blow-away corn bin from Lane Farm with: 'I know about that. Wasn't that.' I didn't have the heart to argue.

After Rue had repeated the episode with more embroidery to Wully and Archie I had, I thought, found a question to sink him.

'Well, if it was as big as you say, what happened to it?'

'Flew to bits,' he retorted instantly. 'They gets bigger and bigger as they go and then, bang, all of a sudden they crumble apart. You go and look near the bottom gate of the Low Meadow you'll see a great ole heap like a drift. Reckon that were it.'

At first I thought Rue was pulling our legs. As he persisted with this extraordinary claim I came to realise he believed it. Perhaps in the brief glimpse of the silo bearing down on him it may have looked like a giant snow ball, particularly if the galvanised finish reflected the snow. Also, as it pressed snow on to him in passing over, he probably thought this had come from the snowbolt. Whatever the reasons, there was no doubt he had convinced himself of a snowbolt and no one was going to persuade him otherwise. What Rue said was right was right.

Being the only person in these parts who had encountered a snowbolt – although he always insisted he knew other folk who had – the experience proved to be extremely useful in that relating it Rue could attract attention, particularly from round-buying strangers in the Anchor. Of course, with the years the tale became more and more exaggerated. The last time I heard snatches of it was a wintry night not long ago when I had gone into the Anchor to collect a few bottles of beer. From the Public Bar Ol' Rue could be heard holding forth in fine fettle: 'There were this noise like thunder and I just has time to look up and see this grut ball a' snow as big as a house. That were comin' at around a hundred mile an hour. I just had time to duck afore that were over me – only missed me by a gnat's foreskin. I thought I was a goner, that took me ten minutes to dig meself out a' the snow . . . Thas the biggest snowbolt I've ever heard tell of.'

I remember thinking that Rue's account was the biggest something else I'd ever heard tell of!

The Seventh Child

Old Rue was never the rural raconteur that old Newson was. For one thing he lacked the mischievous sense of humour his compatriot possessed and frequently used in mockery. Newson's tales nearly always concerned other people whereas Rue talked only of his own experiences, most stories championing his ego. His amorous adventures were a favourite topic, told in blunt fashion. Had his descriptive language come to the ears of the Women's Institute he would certainly have been labelled a dirty old man. His words turned not a hair in the farmyard; save that he did tend to go on about it a lot, the subject was perfectly natural for one so close to the realities of nature. In this respect he was given to exaggeration – or he was otherwise an exceptional man! Such stories, however, were never told just for the sake of being crude, only to affirm his prowess. The particular anecdote that ran favourite in his repertoire was unusual, to say the least, and obviously told with a certain pride.

The introduction was always the same. He would pronounce with an air of satisfaction: 'Well, I fathered seven children in my time but only sired six.' The uninitiated, drawn to the bait, would usually respond to this apparent contradiction with a request for explanation. It is not my intention to tell it here in the graphic form of the usual narrator, although it will be difficult to maintain propriety even with more moderate language and descriptions.

Before myxomatosis decimated the rabbit population in the

early Fifties, the Guv'nor let Rue go round the fields in the evenings with a 12-bore. The Guv'nor provided the shotgun and cartridges, thus diminishing overheads so that Rue could make a bob or two from the rabbits he potted. Being a good shot and knowing where burrows were situated, over the years Rue thinned the rabbits to such an extent that his prey became very wary and required careful stalking. One fine summer evening he was questing along behind a hedge when he saw a teenage boy and girl creeping along the other side. Rue recognised the lad as an 18-year-old who worked on a farm in the next village and the girl as Billy Barnaby's daughter, a nubile hussy of 16 he had often seen hanging around the village street with boys. Rue put two and two together or, more accurately, suspected one and one were intent on coming together. Quietly stalking back down the hedge he watched the youngsters make for a gate into the adjoining field and disappear from view behind a tangled clump of brambles and dog roses that grew in the corner of that hay meadow. As every country person knows, uncut hay meadows make excellent courting grounds because of the cover afforded by long grass and the comfort of old turf. A corn field may provide the cover but the usually hard and cloddy surface is not for lounging on. Thus Rue suspected the couple had gone to ground in the sward and out of sight of his prying eyes. He was just about to resume his quest for rabbits when the sound of giggling made him hesitate. Rue, who knew the hedgerows and fields of the farm as well as the back of his hand, immediately realised where the couple were.

Before the war, back in the early Thirties, when farming was very depressed, the Guv'nor had attempted to help make ends meet by keeping turkeys with an eye on the Christmas market. These were housed free range on this particular meadow in several large poultry sheds. The enterprise did not pay and as there was no sale for the turkey sheds they stood forlornly in the meadow for many years, used chiefly by dairy cows to rub itchy hides against. With the war and the revival of agriculture, the huts were removed and sold, all except one which the cows had partly demolished with their rubbing. This hut was towed and pushed into the corner of the field and there it remained. At some point one end was removed for use of the boards, allowing the roof partly to cave in. Brambles and briars had spread from the adjacent hedges to cover one end while clumps of docks and nettles shielded the other. The giggle had emanated from this spot.

The hedge-lined field boundaries at this point formed a letter T. The ruined turkey house was located hard up against the right-hand corner made by the leg and bar of the T. Rue had been walking along the hedge represented by the bar.

Carefully placing each step so as not to make a noise, Rue slowly progressed towards the tangled corner. A large clump of elder had grown up right beside the broken hut and leafed branches cascaded down over the ditch on Rue's side of the hedge. This canopy so excluded light that little vegetation grew in the ditch beneath, allowing Rue gently to slide down and approach within a couple of feet of the hut side. The original creosote, though faded, still fought off rot in much of the wood cladding but here and there boards had become dislodged by the odd elder branch that had forced a way through. Rue was not long in finding a spy hole; the first peep confirmed his suspicions as to the goings on. What he witnessed in the next few minutes showed that the youngsters were lovers in every sense of the word. Neither was this the first occasion as evidenced by an old coat and a straw-stuffed beet-pulp sack in use as a mattress. Having had his fill, in due time the voyeur stole away as silently as he had come.

The lovers made frequent evening visits to their hideaway during the long summer evenings and just as frequently Rue crept up to watch them. No wonder he often reported a dearth of rabbits. Not a word about this liaison was said to anyone else on the farm during that summer, Rue evidently got much enjoyment from being a Peeping Tom, but felt sufficiently guilty to keep his activities to himself. After he had spied on the lovers for the best part of two months, the novelty began to wear off. But in that devious mind of his Rue started to hatch a plan. There was not much he didn't know about reproductory matters, for taking cows, sows and mares to service had been a regular part of his agricultural life. And there certainly wasn't much he didn't know about similar human activities either. Central to his scheming was the somewhat risky birth control method employed by the young couple which was, to Latinise Rue's colourful description, *coitus interruptus*. Evidently preoccupied with wicked intent for some weeks, by watching and calculating, Rue marked the date for what he planned to do.

As Rue didn't drive a tractor he wasn't much involved in harvesting and rarely did overtime. One fine August evening, while the rest of us were combining and hauling grain, Rue decided the time had come to strike. Seeing the teenagers walking along a hedgerow, Rue tracked them to the ruined turkey shed and watched through a crack in the boards, as he had done many times before. At what he judged was the crucial moment, he pointed his 12-bore into the air and fired off both barrels over the lovers. As he had anticipated, they were, to put it mildly, startled out of their moment of ecstacy. In Rue's words, 'Talk about jump! He wholly drove that home!' Rue smartly hopped out of the ditch and nonchalently walked away to give the impression that he had just taken a pot-shot at a bunny and was quite unaware of the nearby love-nest. Apparently his deception worked – Rue said the lovers deserted the hideway only when the autumn nights began to draw in.

All this was revealed to us one December day when Rue came grinning into the yard in the morning to announce, 'I heared last night the gal Barnaby is gettin' churched!' It was unlike Rue to take an interest in such matters. He was obviously waiting for someone to comment on this fact so I obliged, drawing the response: 'She's pudd'ned; that'll be born on May 9th, you wait and see.' Of course, the next question from all assembled, waiting for the Guv'nor to come out and give the day's orders, was: 'How the hell do you know?' or words to that effect. Then we were treated to a graphic account of what had occurred. Someone commented disdainfully that they thought Rue could have found something better to do than spy on courting couples. To which the voyeur triumphantly responded: 'Ah boy, that made a new man of me. My wife reckoned she been feedin' me too much rich food.'

Naturally, we took all this with a pinch of salt, because Rue did tend to boast. However, word soon spread around the village from another source that the girl Barnaby was having to get married, so Rue was vindicated at least on that score. As the months went by Rue became something of a pain in the neck with his constant progress reports on the expectant mother. Particularly pathetic was his oft-repeated quip that he expected twins were on the way because he had fired twin barrels. I think he went out of the way to mardle with her father in the hope that he might catch a glimpse of the girl. Fortunately for us, the newlyweds, who had lodged at Barnaby's since their wedding day, moved into rented accommodation in the next village early in the spring. While the frequency of Rue's reports was checked he still managed to gain intelligence from some quarter and one morning announced: 'What did I tell yer, thas due in May!' I don't think a doting prospective father could have been more interested. Indeed, Rue somehow came up with a phrase that he had fathered a child by remote control and from then on this was his assumed status in the affair.

As May drew near we were all hoping that the know-all would be proved wrong. When May 9th came with no news of delivery we were all gleefully preparing to take the mickey out of Rue on the following morning. Alas, we were up-staged. Having ingratiated himself with the Barnabys during past months simply to keep abreast of family events, he had used the excuse of dropping in a couple of rabbits on his way to work to learn that their daughter had produced an eight-pound baby boy at 3 o'clock that morning, May 10th.

Insufferable as he was that day, the outcome had made his story the more plausible – although nobody on the farm would admit it to his face. In the years that followed we were now and again treated to such confidences as: 'I see my boy in his pram the other day. Look a bit like me!' or 'They say my seventh child is a growin' apace' or again, 'Him that I blasted into this world has a'started school.'

About six years after their marriage, Barnaby's daughter and her husband parted. There was another child by then and after the divorce custody of both was granted to the mother. Both parties eventually married again and moved away. The mother again had matrimonial problems and went to live with some other man. 'Rue's seventh' and his sister came back to live with their grandparents. Eventually the boy joined the army, news which lent itself to Rue claiming: 'Just what I expected with gunfire bein' in his blood so to speak.' (This despite the fact that the chap was in the Catering Corps.) The last I heard of the lad was that he had married a girl in Aldershot. Rue feigned disappointment: 'He might have asked his old father to the weddin', mightn't he.'

There is an intriguing sidelight to all this. Before the lad joined the army he came to me for a job. At the time I didn't want anybody but I happened to ask him why he had left his previous employment. 'Well', he said, 'I worked over at High Woods turkey farm for a week. Had to leave because of being allergic to that fine dust in the turkey houses.' I never told Rue.

They Don't Make 'Em Like That Any More

Old Newson does love a mardle; although it usually dissolves into a dissertation on the somewhat dubious activities of his acquaintances. Take the afternoon when he came ambling into the farmyard and during the usual exchange of salutations I happened to ask why he was lisping.

'Bit too hard on a peppermint and broke three of the pegs in me top plate,' was the explanation. 'These darned owd National Health's is rubbish – all that plastic they use today. Not like the false teeth they made when they first come out; tough as steel they were; never break. I remember the first set to come around these parts – well, some o' the gentry had 'em before but I'm talkin' about the workin' man's sort.'

'Was there a difference?' I enquired.

'Why yes, hardest thing the gentry ever tackled was a bit of ear nibblin' but a workin' bloke needs a set that'll stand up to bottle-openin' and the like, don't he? Owd Arthur Wrightway had the first workin' man's set in these parts. He use to keep Bucket Hole Farm – oh, that must be fifty or sixty year ago now, long afore your time. Lot of that there gum disease about then; folks was losin' teeth as fast as icicles fall off a roof gutter in a quick thaw.'

'Pyorrhoea,' I volunteered.

'No, no, they was all right that end, it was this here gum rot. Anyway, Arthur's missus, Aggie – she's my cousin – she couldn't abide the sight of him with no gnashers so she nags him into goin' to see a dentist fellow in Ipswich to get a set of these new falsies made. Cost him a small fortune he reckoned, but they were real beauties they were; top and bottom sets hinged together at the back and ivory pegs set in that pretty pink gutta-percha. They don't make 'em like that any more. Strong? Why they was better than a Sheffield shut-knife; one snap of his old chops and he could cut clean through a cart rope. He alus reckoned them teeth was as useful to him as a third hand around the farm. Course, he'd have 'em out once a week – afore Sunday dinner – and sharp 'em up with an old file, just to keep a good edge on 'em. Well, when he first got 'em none round here had seen the like afore and that was the talk of the village. Old gals what met Arthur on the road would say "How about a flash, Mr Wrightway" and he'd bare his gleamers just to give 'em a thrill. Good sport he were. What's more he use to come down to the Rose and Crown of an evenin' and let others try 'em in.'

'That's a bit unhygienic, wasn't it?' I queried.

'Gawd no, boy. They'd swill 'em in a pint of mild after each feller had tried 'em and when all as could had had a go, then Mary the barmaid would polish 'em up with a drop of Brasso to put the shine back. Doubled trade in the tap room they reckoned as fellows come for miles just to try Arthur's teeth. Why owd Hubert Brown even had his last two pegs pulled out just so he could try 'em. Only trouble was he got so excited aforehand that the duddy old fool put 'em in wrong way round and nearly bit his tongue off. Yer know, once Arthur hired 'em out. Time 'Briar' Smith was gettin' wed for the third time. Poor owd boy hadn't got a tooth in his head and you can understand why he wanted to look good for his bride. Arthur swear that every time the church bells rung for a weddin' after he got his teeth back, they got so frisky he thought they were gonna jump right out of his mouth. Course, he was a bit of a ladies' man himself, on the quiet. There was a rare upset once when some gal went home and her mother see a bite mark on her neck. Well, Arthur might just as well have writ his name 'cause there were no mistakin' the mark of his gnashers. Mind you, they was his undoing in the end, yer know.'

'Oh?'

'Time the 'lectricity first come around. Bit through a cable to cut it but that were still live. Arthur didn't know much about it; warped his owd choppers though. They were inclined to stick a bit on the hinges after that.'

'How do you mean, "after that?"?' Curiosity overcame my growing scepticism of this tale.

'Well, Aggie were never one to waste anything and she weren't a goin' to have them lovely set of choppers buried along of Arthur. And good job she didn't 'cause he ain't been in the churchyard more than a couple of months afore she was after marryin' Tommy Leek.'

'Oh yes,' I interjected, 'Wasn't he that little fellow with a face like President Carter's who always looked as if he was on his last legs?'

'You're right there; why they do say as how during the war he volunteered to be a blood donor but when he went they took one look, gave him two pints and sent him home by ambulance. Well, anyways he's another what had had the gum rot so he comes in just right for owd Arthur's beauties. Only thing they was far too big for Tommy. Real struggle to get them in and when they did you should have sin him, why even a Jappy-knees would say he had a mouthful. Still the little owd feller was real proud of them champers, that he was. Never took 'em out, too difficult. Just use to swill a little Jeyes Fluid around his mouth last thing at night to keep things fresh like. Only trouble was his owd jaws weren't really up to working them champers, especially when they'd stick; he'd open his mouth and couldn't shut it. Got him into no end of trouble. Once that happened when he was at market and the auctioneer knocked down three lots to Tommy afore he could get his mouth shut. As the lots happen to be the ducks he'd taken to sell the little feller weren't very pleased. Then there was the time he went to the door and it were the milkman. Them were the days when you could buy milk cheaper if you had it ladled out of a can. Those old milk boys didn't waste any time either; "Where do you want it?" this one asked. The little feller was just a goin' to say he'd get a jug when his champers got stuck wide open. Course, you guessed it; half a pint of skim straight down his gullet. Well, you couldn't blame the milky could yer? Aggie didn't give the little feller any sympathy; not a bit. "You wants to think yourself lucky it weren't the coalman" she say.'

My look of disbelief had no effect upon the narrator who, after a brief pause to pop a peppermint into his mouth, observed: 'Pity the little old feller ain't about today, he'd have made a fortune with them toothpaste firms that advertise on telly. Imagine them grut pair of shining gnashers on yer screen. Mind you, some would think they'd turned on the horror film!'

'He's dead now?'

'Oh yes, been gone ten year or more.' There followed a suitable pause for dramatic effect. 'Mind you, Aggie's still got them teeth.'

'Never!' I protested.

'Yes. Well with her arthritis she have a job to move around and she find if she pop them falsies under her foot she can use 'em to crack nuts or break kindlin' wood. 'Sides, there's a lot of wear left in 'em and you never know when they might come in useful for somebody. I'd have 'em myself if they'd fit.'

There was a suitable pause for effect before his concluding remark. 'Come to think of it, they might be just your size – so if ever your old pegs start appoppin' out you just give me the nod.'

I always take old Newson's yarns with a pinch of salt. But I must admit that for some subconscious reason I'm now being extraordinarily thorough with my toothbrush.

A Purple-Bottomed Spring

'Spring is bursting out all over', runs the song. It certainly is an explosive time of year with everything in nature escaping from the grip of winter. There is also a marked change in animal behaviour, not least man's, of which the worst aspect is the definite satanic stirring in small boys. Perhaps it isn't quite like it was in my day when at this time of year every field, hedgerow and coppice seemed to have a boy or two exploring nature's revival. Nevertheless, come spring today's lad does drag himself away from the goggle-box, in front of which he has been perched all winter, to venture into the leafing lanes. Birds' nests and tadpoles still have their attraction. You can be sure, however, that the activities of today's boy, like yesterday's, cannot rest with simple pleasures. The diabolic pest that lurks within each boy will sooner or later assert itself, as I have from time to time been reminded.

The most memorable occasion was back in the early Seventies. One morning while waiting in the farmyard for the men to arrive for work I saw a robin perch on the farm gate. At least I thought it was a robin, but its lower parts were bright purple. Before I had time to take in the detail the bird fluttered off and I was left wondering whether to phone a naturalist friend to tell him that I had sighted some rare species. Then, within a matter of seconds, I was confronted with the spectacle of a purple-bottomed thrush in a nearby tree. Poor though my ornithological knowledge is, there is no such thing as a purple-bottomed thrush I am sure, and as far as I am aware neither is there in nature a purple-bottomed robin.

The arrival of Tim displaying an outsize bruise across the side of his face distracted my attention from these puzzling birds. 'Hello,' I said, 'What's happened to you? Fallen off your moped?'

Tim, unlike me, is usually very civil first thing in the morning. On this occasion my flippant remark brought forth some expressive epithets coupled with threats of extreme physical action against his next door neighbour's son.

I solicited an explanation. 'Should keep me mouth shut,' he began, 'but my missus thinks it's a hell of a joke so as it'll soon be all over the village I might as well tell you. You know Mrs Whatsit next door to me – her whose husband is in the merchant navy – well, I do her garden for her. Last evening I was puttin' in a couple of rows of peas and she was sat there on a chair having a bit of a natter as she always do. In come that Michael of hers – he's the one about ten with a lot of lip. He's got this grut jam jar full of frog's jelly and when his mother see it she properly kicks up a stink.

'I ain't havin' that horrible stuff here,' she says, 'You go and pour that back in the pond.' The boy he argues back – if he'd bin one of mine I'd have knocked his block off the way he spoke to her. He got in a right temper – runs in the family, yer know. All of a sudden the boy ups with this jar and pours the frog's jelly down the front of his mother's dress. Cor, she damn near had hysterics. 'Get it out, get it out,' she hollers at me. Well, I was a bit taken aback but I started to roll me shirt sleeve up. Then I suddenly thought if anybody sees me . . . what would they think. She's still a hollerin' "Do somethin'. Get this horrible stuff out." So then I had an idea. "Undo the belt of your dress and jump up and down, missus," I says, "perhaps that'll slip out the bottom." '

'Did it?' I enquired.

'No,' said Tim, despondently. 'Tights! Damn stupid things, never ought to have been invented. There she is still screamin' her head off, with a great bulge of frog's jelly trapped over her left ankle. All I could think of was to cut a hole in the leg of her tights to let it flow out but I was just feelin' in my pocket for my pen knife when, whack, right across the side of my head. There's the old gal from across the road settin' about me with a broom! "Leave her alone," she shouts at me. Darn idiot, she'd heard Mrs Whatsit screamin' her head off and thought I was . . . well, we got it all sorted out in the end and there's the old gal and Mrs Whatsit laughin' fit to burst. Well they may, here's me with a sore head and no fault of mine.'

'What happened to the boy?' I enquired in an effort to prevent Tim from indulging in his obvious self-pity as the innocent and aggrieved party.

'Young beggar ran off. I'd have tanned the backside off him when he came back, but she didn't; she's too soft with him.'

At that moment I again beheld the purple-bottomed robin perched on the farm gate. Tim must have followed my incredulous gaze, for to my relief he said: 'That's some more of his doin!'

I asked what he meant.

'That darn boy. Haven't you noticed half the birds round here have all got purple arses? I know it's him 'cause I saw him in the tater shed with some of that dye. He must have been sprinklin' it in every bird's nest he could find.'

Then it dawned on me. The boy had taken one of the old tins of indelible dye crystals we once used for marking stock feed potatoes. A few crystals in a nest; add the damp plumage of the bird and there was the solution to the purple-bottomed bird mystery.

As luck would have it, later that same day I chanced upon young Michael Whatsit and two of his partners-in-crime in one of the farm lanes. They looked apprehensive before a word was said; they looked decidedly frightened when I had finished with them. I was very cross. 'If the rest of that dye isn't returned to me by five o'clock tonight, I'll report you all to the police and the Society for the Protection of Birds.' Well, it sounded good and as the three boys slunk silently away I almost felt a pang of sympathy for them.

We had a heavy shower that afternoon and I got a bit wet before managing to gain the refuge of my old farm van and drive home. When I walked indoors my wife's face lit with amazement: 'What have you been doing? Look at your back!' Yes, the seat of my trousers was purple, the back of my jacket was purple, even my socks were purple. Of course, I did ask the boy to return the rest of the dye, and as I wasn't about I suppose it was natural to pop it in my van. But why did he return the dye in a thin paper bag instead of the original tin he had taken? And why did he choose the driver's seat when placing it in the van?

I have no intention of detailing the extent of the damage to my person but I began to despair of seeing my bath water without its distinctly purple hue. However, there was retribution. When some boy's father returned from his ship he was persuaded to turn another bottom purple — and it wasn't with dye!

Janet's Granny Never Came

The boy wasn't very good at school and at 15 his mother found him a job in the local bakers. He would have preferred to work in a garage or drive a tractor like his old man, but there weren't any vacancies in the locality. The bakehouse was joined to a shop and tea rooms where the produce was dispensed by a staff of women and girls from the village. The boy had not been at work many weeks when he began to take an interest – albeit mild – in a wide-eyed, dark haired little thing who served in the shop and flitted in and out of the bakehouse in the course of collecting more cakes. Her lack of height and disproportionate curves barred her from being called pretty, but a warm personality bubbled out with her broad country words and made her popular with all on the premises. The boy's interest arose because Janet always talked to him as if he mattered; not that they ever had any real conversation. She would say: 'Are them buns ready for me yet?' in a warm friendly way that contrasted with the snappy remarks and orders of the bakers and the women.

Once, when the baker had rebuked the boy in Janet's presence with 'Keep that bloody great mop of hair out of the dough; we ain't making wattle and daub,' she had whispered consolingly as she went out of the door: 'Nasty old man. I think you've got nice hair.' However, the boy's desire was nurtured from afar for his fancy for Janet engendered an awkward shyness and he was unable to engage in imaginative conversation.

One morning when the boy was greasing tins he overheard some of the women talking about Janet in the next room. Most of the conversation was unintelligible because over it the baker was singing his own wrong-word version of some top-of-the-pops melody. But the boy did hear a woman call through to another in the shop. 'Did you hear that, Martha? Janet's granny hasn't come.' He could not quite catch the reply, but the first woman added: 'Poor gal is somethin' worried about it. No wonder she ain't bin to work for a couple of days.' The boy pondered these words as he half-heartedly dabbed the grease around the tins. He finally concluded that Janet's granny must have been going to stay with her but had been taken ill. Poor Janet, she must be very fond of her granny to be so upset.

Janet was at work the following day, but not the next. Concerned for his secret fancy the boy enquired of one of the women in the shop: 'Did Janet's granny come to see her?' The woman looked somewhat amazed and was obviously lost for an answer. Feeling he had not made himself clear, the boy went on 'I thought I heard you say her granny was coming to stay or somethin' and Janet was worried 'cause she didn't turn up. Is she ill?'

'Oh yes, Janet is something worried about her poor granny, the old lady's somethin' ill I hear,' the woman replied, though with a distinct lack of solemnity. Then she turned to another woman for support; 'Isn't that right, Martha?'

'Oh yes,' said Martha, who could hardly contain herself with mirth – although the boy did not notice this – 'poor Janet is something troubled 'cause her granny ain't come.' At that moment the baker could be heard loudly demanding: 'Where's that bloody boy now. Always missing when he's wanted.' So the conversation was abruptly terminated and in his urgency to get back to the bakehouse the boy must have overlooked the hilarious female laughter that followed his departure from the shop.

Although Janet's indisposition apparently passed, the boy did not have much opportunity to speak to her at work but he was determined to enquire about her grandmother's health at the first opportunity. Even though he was usually lost for conversation, he could manage a direct question. Janet, being two years his senior, worked an hour longer than he but there came an occasion when she left early and happened to be pushing her cycle out onto the road at the same time as the boy emerged from the bakery building with his.

'Is your granny better now, Janet?' he stammered.

'My granny?' queried Janet.

'She's bin ill ain't she?' said the boy.

'Why, both my grannies have been dead for years,' she said kindly.

'Oh, I must have heard wrong,' the boy mumbled and, red-faced, pedalled off as fast as his chopper would take him.

A few days after that, word spread through the bakehouse that Janet was getting married – quickly. 'She's got herself pudd'nd' explained the baker. The boy was heartbroken, – he had known nothing of Janet's associations with the opposite sex but, as happens with the young, his emotions were soon healed.

He was lounging on the corner outside the pub on the June Saturday when Janet arrived at the church in purest white. He watched with his mates as the little crowd threw confetti outside the church door and the white-sashed taxi whisked the happy couple away.

'Thas Janet Dottin's gettin' married ain't it?' remarked one of the youths.

'Yah,' replied another.

'Who's she marryin'?' enquired the first.

'Jerry Hodge, that long streak of piss from Wickham who think he know it all. Can't see what she found in him.'

'Nice gal, Janet.' One youth addressed the boy. 'She worked at your place didn't she?'

'Yah' said the boy, swinging a leg and kicking the kerbstone as he lounged across his bike. 'Them old women down there they told me Janet's grandma was ill, but when I asked her she said she ain't got any now. Bloody ol' women, properly made me feel a fool.'

But not half such a fool as he would one day feel when he understood a little more about women and their ways.

The Little Old Lady

The motor car, more than any other factor, was responsible for the dramatic changes in village life which occurred in the mid-20th century. In the Thirties the hamlet around our farm was occupied exclusively by people whose occupations were based in the parish. Now, by courtesy of the motor car, the farm labourers, carpenters and the like are gone and every cottage has been transformed into a commuter's home. The place is now a dormitory for professional people who work in Ipswich, Colchester and London. Speedy communication has also brought the demise of many village shops; today it's into the car and away to the cut-price supermarket in the nearest town. Not that some of the smaller country shop-keepers made much of a living before supermarkets came on the scene.

Our hamlet was for many years served by a shop that was run by a little old lady. Both premises and owner appeared to be left-overs from Edwardian times. The shop stood in isolation from neigh-bouring houses, fronting the road beside a clump of elms. Un-usually, the upstairs windows in the thatched roof had wooden shutters and these always seemed to be closed. The bow-fronted display window was anything but enticing, having nothing more than a few faded display cards, prominent among which was a large one for Epsom Salts. The display was often enhanced by a big black and white cat curled up and sleeping. Occasionally we were treated to more variety when the cat would deposit there the

remains of a sparrow or mouse it had caught while out hunting.

When the brown-painted door of the shop was opened a coiled-spring bell fixed to its inner side was set ringing. This summoned the shopkeeper, but before she arrived from a curtained doorway in the back there was ample time to survey the scene which, in more than 20 years that I patronised the place, underwent no obvious changes. Confronting you on entering the shop was a 40-inch-high board counter painted in the same faded brown as the door. At one end of the counter was a large set of balance scales from which much of the enamel had long been worn away by constant use. Beside the scales sat a neat pile of balance weights and to the right was an open space for serving customers. Along the front of the rest of the counter stood a row of large screw-top glass jars filled with an assortment of brightly coloured boiled sweets and toffees. The walls behind the counter supported numerous shelves stocked with cigarettes, tobacco, tins of cocoa, jars of jam, tea and other packaged groceries. Against one side wall a bank of small drawers stretched from floor to ceiling, there being no external indication whatsoever of their contents. The other side wall was festooned with hanging objects; stove kettles, saucepans, oil lamps and odd items of ironmongery for which there can have been little call.

The proprietress of this establishment was as quaint as the property and its contents. After never less than a full minute a rustling could be heard as the curtain was drawn slowly aside to reveal an Edwardian apparition. A white lace bonnet framed a small rounded face from which grey eyes peered over the top of fine framed spectacles; always over, never through, in my observations. The dress was black or navy blue – it was hard to tell – but most certainly of Edwardian origin, with a high neck and billowing folds at bosom and waist. The only concession to seasonal change was a white shawl draped around the shoulders if the weather was chill. Black wool mittens were discarded only on the hottest of days. I do not recall her ever wearing anything else but this sort of dress; even on Sundays the white bonnet could be seen at the back of the church – viewed from the choir stalls she looked just like Mrs Tiggywinkle of the Beatrix Potter illustrations.

My earliest memory of Miss Gentry is of that bonneted head peering down at me over the very high counter and enquiring: 'What will it be today, young man?' ''

It was always the same salutation, even if you went into the shop twice in one day; from which I conclude she never troubled to distinguish between any of the half-dozen small boys who patronised the place for a penn'orth of sweets. When deciding what sort of sweets to buy there was a natural inclination to touch the selected jar when indicating your decision. This immediately provoked a gentle smack on the head and a curt: 'Fingers off the jars now.'

The smack was administered with what looked like a small square of soft carpet tied to the end of a toasting fork – a specially devised weapon no doubt. The first smack was not much more than a tap, but if you persisted in finger-marking the jars the weapon was wielded with more severity. As the unlabelled sweet jars were arranged along the front of the counter and unnecessarily exposed to juvenile fingering, I suspect Miss Gentry derived some slight sadistic pleasure from wielding her swat.

There were other goodies such as sugar mice, liquorice coils and sherbet dabs in boxes on the counter, hidden behind the jars and out of view until you grew to be 11 or 12. Hygiene doesn't usually bother small boys, but looking back I recall that Miss Gentry's cat was often asleep on the sherbet dabs and you could sometimes find fly dirt on the sugar mice. Asking, say, for a lime lollipop, did not mean prompt exchange for your halfpenny. Various other sweet-meats would first be held up to view with an enquiry: 'This?' On reflection I think Miss Gentry enjoyed our impatient protestations, for this happened so frequently as to become an expected ritual endured to obtain what you wanted.

Quick service was something unknown in Miss Gentry's shop. Her every action was slow and methodical; the small triangular paper bag into which a hap'porth of acid drops was shovelled was never passed over the counter unless the top had been folded to make a flap and carefully tucked in. The supreme time-consumer was the acquisition of a reel of thread or card of elastic for one's mother. Such items reposed in the nest of drawers against the side wall, requiring the careful positioning of a step-ladder and the even more careful placing of feet upon it. On such occasions you were treated to a flash view of laced black boots under the ample skirt.

Even in my childhood days Miss Gentry cannot have made much of a living, for patronage of her shop was usually limited to the folk in our hamlet. In later years she probably only took enough to pay rates and other overheads and we assumed her pension kept her going. By the 1950s Miss Gentry was something of an anachronism, so much had society changed. I felt sorry for her and now and again would pop into the shop to make the odd purchase. Her stock phrase of 'What will it be today?' did lose the 'young man' suffix when I had grown sufficiently above the shop counter to look down on her, but even after a near quarter century of patronage she still maintained her chosen propriety towards her customers. The shop counter was a point of demarkation and only matters of trade were discussed over it. Nor, as far as I am aware, did she have any friends or social life in the village. Apart from church, the only occasion I recall seeing her away from the shop was the first Thursday in every month when she caught the bus to town.

Sometime early in the Sixties Miss Gentry bowed out. She was 88 and was found dead in the shop by a customer. The burial was not local and soon afterwards the shop was sold to become a private house. It was sad to see this change, for Gentry's shop had been a feature of village life for as long as I could remember. There was sorrow too for the little old lady who seemed so isolated in the mid-20th century.

Perhaps a decade after her passing I was astonished to learn from our retired local bobby that Miss Gentry wasn't quite what she seemed. During one of those nostalgic exchanges in which long-time residents of a village delight, I made a sympathetic comment about Miss Gentry's years of business with such poor return. This was greeted with amusement and the startling information that Miss Gentry was a very wealthy woman. She had been married twice and owned a large West End store plus a clothing factory in Barnsley – the latter inherited from the second husband. Up until her dying day she maintained a large house and staff near Chelmsford under her married name. She inspected this establishment regularly, on the first Thursday of each month, while the rest of the time she lived almost as a recluse under her maiden name. My informant knew all this because on her death he had been called to the shop and had had to trace her next-of-kin. Upstairs he had found beautifully kept financial records of the London and Barnsley businesses, which were administered by a nephew. There was no doubt, however, who held the purse strings.

For me it was all a bit hard to equate with the old fashioned shopkeeper I had known. Had she become something of a recluse as the result of losing two husbands? Our retired constable didn't know how the first husband had died, but the second had seemingly been struck on the head by a length of guttering that fell from the house. 'There were suspicious circumstances,' the constable added, 'but of course it was ridiculous; you can't imagine a little lady like Miss Gentry clobbering anyone on the head, can you?'

'No,' I replied, not very convincingly.

A Pastoral Encounter with Clinging Results

It has always been my contention that the countryside is far more exciting than the urban scene and that in it there is rarely a dull moment. Even so, some moments can become a bit too unnerving for my liking. Take one sunny afternoon a couple of summers ago. There was I ambling along the side of a meadow, nibbling at the stem of a piece of bent grass while pondering some agricultural problem. Suddenly this peaceful pastoral scene was peaceful no longer. Around a bend in the hedgerow appeared a youngish woman running like the unproverbial clappers. I just had time to notice she was clad in slacks and an anorak and was clutching a haversack in one hand before she literally threw herself upon me.

Now I've heard about men who have an overpowering attraction for women, but I'm definitely not one of them. There was that party last Christmas where some little lovely threw her arms around my neck and cooed in my ear, but as she kept calling me Donald it was obvious she was under such a cloud of alcoholic inebriation she would not have been able to tell an octogenarian from her boyfriend.

But to return to the extraordinary encounter in the meadow. While this sort of thing certainly does powers for the ego when you're the wrong side of 50, there just had to be an explanation. In this case it was very evident that the young woman was absolutely terrified. Still clutching my arm she eventually managed to regain enough breath to stammer: 'You must help us. They're after us. They've got Lucy.'

Obviously Lucy was in dire peril and as I set off down the meadow with the frightened girl following, my mind strove to find a reason for their predicament. As far as I was aware the only people in the vicinity were our two pensioners who were hand-hoeing sugar beet in the next field. They always talked as if they were a couple of old lechers, but the big talkers are usually the safe ones. Dammit, they're both in their seventies; or had they run amok? I visualised a headline in the *News of the World* on Sunday. It was therefore with some relief that, on reaching the brow of the hill, I beheld another terrified girl attempting to keep a small tree between herself and a bunch of young heifers.

The first girl was now clinging to my coat sleeve again. 'We were walking along the footpath when all those bulls came rushing towards us. I thought we were going to be killed,' she panted.

'They're not bulls, they're young heifers,' I corrected.

'They're bulls; they came running down the hill at us; it was terrible.' I had no intention of explaining the difference between bulls and heifers and decided to play my trump card. 'Look, I'm the farmer. You take it from me they are heifers. They won't hurt you. The only reason they ran towards you is because they're friendly and they like human company.'

From the way she continued to hang on to my sleeve as we approached her beseiged companion she obviously didn't believe a word. I waved my free arm and shouted a few 'Go on's' to the animals. Some unwillingly moved aside and the other girl, seeing her chance, bolted out from behind the tree. She grabbed hold of my arm with such force that I was knocked off balance and the three of us ended up in a heap on the grass.

'Now look,' I said as sternly as I could, 'for heaven's sake stop worrying. They won't hurt you.' But by the time I had disentangled myself from a haversack strap and staggered to my feet both girls had re-attached themselves to my coat sleeves like leeches. 'Okay,' I said, 'I'll take you to the top gate.'

At first it was a difficult journey, because the hikers were all the time looking back at the heifers. Luckily the animals only followed a short distance and then stood in a bunch and watched us depart, obviously bewildered by the theatricals their presence had caused.

'You are obviously not used to cattle,' I suggested. 'Oh yes,' said one of the clingers, 'we've been through lots of fields of cows, but cows don't come after you. You won't get us going into fields where there are bulls again.' I didn't bother to correct her, because by that time we had rounded the bend in the hedge and I was aware we had a spectator. Standing by the gate was a representative of a local corn merchant – obviously seeking me. He had a look that could have been either mild amazement or slight embarrassment, the significance of which did not immediately register with me. The girls still hung on, taking furtive glances over their shoulders, and did not release their grip until through the gate, which the representative had opened for us. Relief was obvious in their smiling faces. 'Oh thank you so much,' said one 'You were wonderful.'

'Yes, I don't know what we'd have done without you,' said the other. 'Oh it was nothing,' I countered, as they set off up the lane.

Turning to the rep I suddenly became aware of his somewhat incredulous expression. 'They're hikers. The heifers ran after

them. They were terrified.' I tried to say it in a matter-of-fact way, but the implication of his expression had caused my cheeks to flush. 'We've got a very good buy in fertiliser you may be interested in,' he said, pointedly ignoring my remarks.

I gave him an order. But I have a nasty feeling it wasn't because his fertiliser was a good buy.

Romantic Lure of
The No Through Road

Of several unmade country lanes in our district there is no question that Friars Lane is the most picturesque. More by fortune than design it remains much the same as 40 or 50 years ago. We who farm the fields on either side never seem to have time to wage war on the tangle of vegetation that marks the lane's zig-zag route across three hills and two valleys.

Added to this is our reluctance to interfere with a place that in childhood days was a wonderful adventure playground. Then the order of every bush and tree in those unruly hedges was known. Elder stubs from which to fashion pop-guns, hazels that grew fat cob nuts, great sprawls of dog roses in which the brave built secret hideouts. There was even a hollow oak which one could enter at the base and climb up inside the trunk to make ghostly wails that scared the living daylights out of unsuspecting passers-by.

Friars Lane was once firm enough for a six-horse team to draw a wagon of corn from one end to the other. But with the metalling of roads alternative routes were preferred and only at the two ends, which are lined with a few houses, has the council maintained the surface.

Thus nature has been given almost free rein, and but for the passage of an occasional farm tractor or pedestrian, Friars Lane is a deserted wilderness.

That is, it was until a few years ago when the local council

decided to erect at either end a simple but apparently inviting sign –
NO THROUGH ROAD.

For a considerable number of motorists a No Through Road is a
challenge. These fall into three main categories. The first are the
disbelievers, so-called because they are unable to accept the notice
as fact. The disbelievers have, over the years, driven a varied
assortment of vehicles into the lane's narrow ways. Trapped,
unable to move, they have had to be rescued by tractor and cable.
While most have been sports cars piloted by questing young men,
the bag includes an articulated lorry, two army bren-gun carriers
and a recovery vehicle. As the army's unsuccessful assault was
launched in mid-winter there may be some truth in the story that
one of the bren gun carriers sank from sight in the mire.

The second group of motorists
who appear in Friars Lane consists
of picnic addicts. Usually they just
sit in their cars and munch, but
occasionally a few of the more agile
venture forth. One summer I
chanced to come across two
middle-aged couples seated round a
folding table a good 20 yards out in
a field of barley. Repressing the
expletives that all too readily
sprang to mind, I calmly asked if
they would mind removing them-
selves to a more suitable place. They were convulsed with laughter
at their error. It was hard to appreciate the joke, the barley being a
foot high and almost ready to harvest!

The third, and by far the largest, body of motorist visitors to
Friars Lane I can only class as lovers – lacking a safer descriptive
word. I have never read the *Kama Sutra* but I feel the opening line of
a revised version should read: 'First find yourself a No Through
Road.'

Winter and summer there always seems to be a couple closeted
in a car down there. The occupants seem highly indignant when

you have to cough loudly and politely ask them to move so that you can pass with a tractor they should have heard coming a mile away. Occasionally coughing isn't enough, and you need to bang on the steamed-up windows. On a warm summer's day the contestants will venture out of their cars and, unfortunately, into the adjoining barley fields. The area of standing barley two amorous humans can roll down is considerable, if variable. But in the course of the past ten years the total rolled must easily amount to an acre. Under 'Crop failures – please give cause of loss' on the Ministry harvesting form, I have been sorely tempted to enter 'Flattened by fornication, 0.05 acre.' Not that I think Ministry officials would be shocked. It's just that one doesn't know what ideas it might give them.

In fact the popularity of Friars Lane leads me to wonder if it couldn't become a better financial proposition than farming. Competitive events for motorists, like the RAC rally, would be child's play compared with this. How about a sign reading: 'Have a 50-pence frolic in our barley. Special ticklish varieties grown.' Or could I be prosecuted for keeping a bawdy barley field?

Nasty

I have already recounted one episode concerning Nasty, the incorrigible rogue my father employed for a year or so. This account of a later happening shows another vindictive side of this character, and suggests the sort of conduct that brought him his strange nickname.

The year was 1947 or 1948. It was autumn. There had been drought conditions during the summer and by late October little grazing was left for the steers on the 'off farm', which consisted of some twenty-five acres of water meadows and an isolated stock-yard with buildings at the end of a lane off the road to our village. The Guv'nor had given Nasty and me the regular job of feeding wilted sugar-beet tops to the steers to make up for the grazing deficiency. We carried out our task first thing in the morning and last thing before 'knocking off time' in the late afternoon. The job did not really need two people and I suspect that I was there to ensure that Nasty didn't arrive late to work or slope off early. However, both of us were happy to pretend that the job of carrying forkfuls of tops from the heap beside the buildings to mangers in the yard required at least a half-hour to perform. In fact, it took no more than ten minutes. The rest of the time was spent loafing, particularly in the afternoon, when Nasty would lean on the handle of his four-tine fork and make derisive comments about somebody or something, while at intervals removing and consulting the large chained watch from his waistcoat pocket, lest he should spend one second too much in the Guv'nor's service.

It was during one of these loafing periods as the shadows deepened that Nasty's attention was drawn to pheasants making for a thicket at the top of the hill on the northern side of the valley. The thicket was actually a neglected vegetable garden and orchard at the back of a house. Before Hitler's war and the advent of planning restrictions, two desirable residences had been built along the road crowning the hill, undoubtedly located for the view they provided. At the outbreak of war the family in one had fled to the West Country never to return, and the house was later commandeered by the army. The large garden, however, remained unattended and a wilderness was gradually established. About two years after the end of hostilities the property was purchased by a middle-aged retired naval commander. This industrious man began an assault on his unruly garden but his progress was slow and was at first concentrated on the area fronting the house. The other, adjoining, property had always been well maintained and it had changed hands on several occasions. At the time of this tale it was occupied by two ladies who worked for a London publishing company and used the house as a weekend country retreat.

But to return to Nasty and the pheasants. As the birds were seen on a number of occasions it was apparent that the garden thicket was their roost. To Nasty, noted for his poaching prowess, this roost became a nagging obsession worth regular speculation on how easy it would be to take a few brace. For want of something better to do I would argue with him on this point. Nasty was always so boastful it was a natural reaction to counter his egotism with ridicule, not that it ever had any dampening effect.

Finally, one afternoon Nasty announced that he was going to have a go; the clocks had 'gone back' and he would have the full cover of darkness by around a quarter past five. As the venture had evolved into what amounted to a challenge, I found myself having to wait on the result when I would have much rather been off home. Reluctantly I hovered around the farm buildings while Nasty set off. I watched him cross the low meadow, climb the far gate and begin ascending the hill, keeping close to a hedgerow. Soon he was lost in the shadows. All was silent; not a breath of breeze. The sinking sun flecked the horizon clouds with crimson.

I strained my eyes towards the thicket but could make out no movement; the thicket had in any case become part of the general dark shape of the hillside as night advanced. The expectation was an alarm cry of disturbed pheasants fluttering away into the gloom. But still nothing stirred. Time dragged by; I was mentally debating whether or not to go home to tea, but I knew that if I was not present when Nasty returned, he would be bound to claim success next day. Just as the thought occurred that he was deliberately prolonging his empty-handed return so that I would become fed up with waiting and go home, a dark shape materialised from the gloom of the low meadow. As he climbed the yard gate I could see Nasty was carrying nothing. I was about to chide him when he said: 'Shine yer bike torch here, boy.' There was triumph in his voice. The torch revealed Nasty with jacket open and two large cock pheasants, their necks secured with binder twine, looped around the back of his neck.

'What about them then? And there's more!'

My only recourse was to complain about his long absence,

which he simply ignored, continuing to enjoy his winning streak.

'Place is runnin' with rabbits too, so I put down a few wires' he confided in lowered voice, as if a poaching competitor might be listening nearby. Nasty always carried snares in his pocket and never missed a chance to set one in a likely looking run. In fact, if the Guv'nor had been aware of the amount of time given over to snare setting during working hours Nasty would have been out of a job. As we pedalled out of the lane Nasty directed: 'Don't you go tellin' anyone about this. I'm gonna have some more of them fellas out of there.'

The following day the vet came to cut some pigs. As usual he was late. He could never pass our local pub at opening time without taking the opportunity to obtain a little liquid support. The evidence was always on his breath in the confined space of the sty. As one of the hands required to hold the piglets for his knife, I did not take kindly to being made half an hour late for my lunch because of his indulgence. On this particular occasion, it meant also that as I ate in the farm kitchen I was inflicted with the constant chatter of my mother's 'help', Mrs Keswick, who came on Friday afternoons. Mrs Keswick also came on Tuesday mornings and while her ability with a duster and polish was undeniable, she never faltered in her flow of village news and comment acquired at her numerous other charring jobs. Friday afternoons were particularly vocal, because we heard then the intelligence she had gathered at the doctor's house where she charred in the morning. My mother made mild complaints about Mrs Keswick's verbal diarrhoea to the rest of my family, but I suspect she was not averse to listening to the odd piece of juicy gossip. Certainly it always seemed that mother stayed near Mrs Keswick, although Mrs Keswick was happy to continue her talk when she was two rooms away from her listener. My mother was rarely heard to contribute to the conversation anything more than a regular flow of acknowledgements such as 'Really?', 'Well I never!', 'Oh!', 'Hmmm!' 'Did she?', 'Good Heavens!' No one was starved of conversation when Mrs Keswick was about – if you could get a word in.

On this particular Friday, while I was putting away over-cooked toad-in-the-hole, Mrs Keswick was polishing in the sitting room and my mother was popping in and out of the kitchen in the course of some domestic chore. I wasn't really paying any attention until my mother exclaimed 'A snare!' as she came in and went to a cupboard. I stopped crumping on a mouthful of crisp batter, curious as to why a snare featured in the diatribe. Mentally switching on to Mrs Keswick's chatter I became very interested at what I heard:

'. . . that back garden of his ain't been touched for years has it?' (Mother: 'No') 'Anyroad, seems how he heard something down there the night before so he thought he'd have a look round. Tha's when it happened. Goes over front'eds onto a gooseberry bush – right around here.' My mother was obviously treated to a visual indication of the approximate area of body involved, but as the final part of the statement had been in hushed tones I had a pretty good idea what was being demonstrated in the next room.

Mrs Keswick continued in lowered voice: 'You wouldn't believe the tender places the doctor had to pull prickles out of – you know how long they are on an old gooseberry bush?' (Mother: 'Ouch!') 'Reckon he'll be sore for weeks. 'Course, he's grumpy enough at best of times so heaven knows what he'll be like now . . .'

Mrs Keswick moved on to another topic, but I had heard enough to identify the subject of the gooseberry-bush incident as Commander Cruikshank. Whether or not Mrs Keswick had eavesdropped on Doctor Gates telling his wife, or whether Mrs Gates had rashly passed on what her husband had, unprofessionally perhaps, told her, was open to speculation. But to me it appeared that the Commander had caught a foot in one of Nasty's wires and as a result of tumbling into a mass of thorns had to seek the services of our local doctor to remove those that were retained in his person. In turn, I would delight in telling Nasty of what I immediately thought of as a highly amusing additional outcome of his poaching venture.

After lunch the Guv'nor sent me to take a horse to be shod at the blacksmiths. On the way it occurred to me that Commander Cruikshank would not have found the incident at all amusing and might well be intent on apprehending the culprit who had set snares in his back garden. The more I thought about it the more anxious I became to warn Nasty, but I had to wait for the blacksmith to finish shoeing somebody else's horse and it was nearly dark by the time I got back to the farm. Hopping on my bike, I pedalled furiously down to the off-farm. Nasty's bike was propped against the wall of a shed but there was no sign of him, even though we were ten minutes from knocking-off time. Obviously he had slipped off early to try and pick up some more pheasants and check his snares. An overcast had brought darkness earlier and I could discern little through the gloom beyond the other side of the low meadow. Suddenly there was a flash and report from the top of the hill. Then another. My immediate reaction was one of horror that Nasty should be so foolish as to use a gun on the pheasants. That notion did not last long; the flashes were directed from inside the Commander's wilderness. He was shooting at Nasty! Further rationalisation brought the view that the Commander had been shooting up into the air to frighten the invader off his property.

This time I did not have to wait long before a shape, moving at some speed, appeared from the darkness of the bottom meadow. 'Nasty?' I hissed.

'The old bugger shot me,' came the breathless response.

I took the torch from my bike and followed Nasty into the barn. Illumination revealed a somewhat shaken, torn and bleeding Nasty who, between gasps for breath, uttered four-letter-word abuse at his supposed assailant and swore that he had been mortally wounded. A survey of Nasty's person with the torch revealed numerous tears to the front of his trousers and jacket, scratched and bleeding hands and a bloody face, all quite clearly caused by barbed wire and bushes. There was no damage to his back. I offered the opinion that he had sustained his wounds through his hasty exit from the garden, from bushes and cattle fencing rather than from shotgun pellets. Nasty, who was really a terrible coward, was unwilling to accept this view and persisted in claiming that he had been shot and that the Commander had been trying to kill him. That being the case, I suggested, surely the Commander would be in hot pursuit to finish the job. Nasty evidently decided to take this jibe seriously, for he was out of the barn and away on his bike with a speed one would hardly believe possible of a man who was mortally wounded.

Nasty did not appear at work on Saturday morning. I cannot now remember what feeble excuse he sent the Guv'nor – not that there was anything unusual in his failure to turn up as he had at best a very casual attitude to regular employment. I fully expected our local bobby to appear and start asking questions but evidently the Commander was content to deal with the business in his own explosive way. Nasty did come to work on the following Monday, still maintaining to me that he had been shot and muttering threats about getting even with the Commander. He probably realised that he had just been frightened off, but being Nasty he was not going to admit it. However, he was wise enough not to moan to anyone else on the farm about the assumed assault, probably because he knew he would have been laughed at. I thought that the matter would now rest and that Nasty's vindictive threats were just so much hot air. But I was wrong. One Monday morning about three weeks later the village bobby arrived at the farm: had we seen anyone acting suspiciously in the neighbourhood of Commander Cruikshank's house? No, we hadn't; so he left. The Guv'nor, ever a confidante of our bobby, had the full story. Apparently the ladies who lived in the house next to the Commander's had returned from their regular Sunday morning walk at about 11.30 to find all the washing missing from their clothes line. The ladies noticed one of the garments caught on the dividing fence between their garden and the Commander's, further investigation revealing other bits of laundry on his lawn. The ladies stomped round to protest but the Commander was not yet back from morning service, at which he regularly officiated as a sidesman. To their anger and indignation they then spied a quantity of their underwear reposing on a table in the Commander's kitchen. At that point the gentleman returned home and was confronted by the two women with accusations of perversion. As a decidedly straight heterosexual individual who had divorced three wives in his time, the Commander countered with some pretty strong naval language inadvertently questioning the parent-hood of the ladies. This provoked one lady into striking the Commander several times with a rolled umbrella whereupon, in self-defence, he grabbed her in the chest and pushed her away. The other lady, springing to the defence of her friend, attempted to kick the Commander in the groin while delivering a flow of invective more appropriate to the quarter-deck than a Suffolk garden. The combatants then withdrew to telephone the police and protest assault. Tempers had cooled by the time our local pillar of the law arrived to investigate. It did not take him long to discover that the clothing on the kitchen table had been squeezed through the window light and that the blurred footprints in the flowerbed below the window were definitely made by large hob-nailed boots on feet much bigger than the Commander's. His deduction was that someone wanting to create mischief, knowing both sets of householders to be absent, had transferred the washing from the line to next door's kitchen. The parties did not prefer charges of assault, the Commander explaining that he had not intended to grab the lady's chest but rather the umbrella she was wielding. For her part the other lady said it was purely an accident that she had kicked the Commander in the groin when running to aid her friend.

I suspect from his questions that the Guv'nor thought I knew something about this business, probably because I over acted my innocence. As for Nasty, his reaction at the recounting of this altercation among gentlefolk was so negative as to be damning. 'Don't know nothin' about it, boy,' he would blandly say to shrug off my attempts to gain a confession. I could, however, pretty well guess what had happened. No doubt Nasty had been on the road, seen the ladies setting out for their morning constitutional and then passed the Commander heading for church. When he got to their houses he saw the washing and seized the opportunity to get his own back. The nearest I ever got to extracting an admission of his involvement was by fibbing that the bobby had been round to the Guv'nor saying the CID had found fingerprints on the Commander's kitchen window. Nasty looked a bit sheepish and snapped: 'Well, can't have been mine 'cause I allus wear gloves on a Sunday.'

Nasty didn't work for the Guv'nor for very long after that. He found an easier way to make a living. The Welfare State was his eventual salvation from work. Last I heard was that he had developed a persistent bad back and moved in with a widow in Bury St. Edmunds.

Edie

Edie Mortlake was our village tart, as her mother and grand-mother had been before her.

Edie began to establish her reputation at a very early age. When she was nine she was found examining a small boy in the school lavatory. The headmistress administered the cane to those errant hands and severely chastised the child for such sinful practice. A year later another little boy was surprised by his mother in the act of examining Edie in a garden shed. This time it was the boy who underwent punishment, for the irate parents could not conceive that the little girl was anything but innocent.

Edie's school days were prematurely and abruptly terminated during her fifteenth year, following a botany ramble when she and one of the bigger boys demonstrated a greater interest in biology. Their schoolmistress realised she had lost two pupils in the wood and, when she found them, discovered that Edie had lost something else. Although the girl was below the age of consent, the vicar and school governors were frightened of the adverse publicity a court case would bring the village. As a result the matter was hushed up and dealt with by expulsion of the wayward youngsters after a severe lecture on the perils of such dreadful behaviour.

As an act of social conscience, one of the school governors, a retired city gentleman, employed Edie as a kitchen maid. If he had hopes his household would be a good influence on this fallen girl he was soon to be disillusioned. Edie's nubile charms and her insatiable appetite for male company had the inevitable result. Her employer began to notice that her curves were becoming more than ample in one area and his worst fears were soon confirmed. The village gossip 'hot line' carried the news that 'Edie Mortlake's puddin'd.' As was the custom in the moralising society of those times – 1930 to be precise – the vicar arrived to elicit the father's name from Edie with a view to suggesting a hasty marriage. The poor man was much taken aback and gave up in disgust on discovering there were no less than five contenders to the title. So it happened that two weeks from her seventeenth birthday Edie produced a fine baby boy, thus affording the village women the delight of speculation as to the identity of the father for many years to come.

It must be said of Edie that she was of pleasant nature and happy disposition. She was kind-hearted and generous. She was also shrewd enough to appreciate that she could swap her favours for rent-free accommodation, groceries and a hundredweight of coal a week. The first of these benefits was bestowed by a bachelor

builder who was more than old enough to be her father. As landlord of the Mortlake's cottage he called one day to take down measurements for a replacement door. It seems that these were not the only things taken down and thereafter, whenever Mr and Mrs Mortlake were absent, the builder arrived to inspect the premises. Such an arrangement was fraught with difficulty and before long Edie and her child were offered accommodation in another property of the builder's that had become vacant.

The builder, a sidesman and parish councillor, was the master of discretion, always parking his van in the pub yard and having a quick half before stealing across a meadow to Edie's. The secrecy was prompted by the belief that his trade would suffer should his more puritanical customers get to hear of his association with such a loose girl. Fear of discovery and business demands on his time limited the builder's visits to one or two evenings a week. Edie, however, was soon happily responding to the advances of the grocer and the coalman, whose visits occupied the remaining nights of her week. She kept each man in ignorance of her associations with the others, but she wisely pretended to the grocer and coalman that she had a fiance, the better to hasten their departure should the builder arrive unexpectedly. And, sure enough, one night he did.

During a clandestine visit of the coalman, Edie heard a key in the kitchen door. The coalman was hurriedly ushered out of the bedroom window onto the adjoining coalshed roof, an escape route previously devised for such emergencies. Regrettably, the rotten state of the timbers in the coalshed roof had not been ascertained. The weight of the portly coalman proved too much and with a resounding crash of breaking tiles and timbers he hurtled through to land on his own droppings, so to speak. As the alarmed builder emerged from the kitchen door, the black and bleeding coalman fled by him, stammering the breathless explanation: 'Just been making a late delivery.' Fortunately, in the half-light the builder failed to recognise the figure or to notice it was trouserless. Being of a trusting nature he jumped to the conclusion that a Peeping Tom had been trying to spy into Edie's bedroom. Edie, naturally, did not disillusion him. When the builder's men repaired the coalshed roof he had them cement broken glass round the edges. Luckily, Edie never had to ask any of her lovers to use that escape route again. As for the coalman, his ardour was evidently quenched by this experience and by having to explain his injuries and lack of trousers to an irate wife.

Not long after this episode Edie was deserted also by the grocer. She became pregnant again and he had no stomach for a paternity suit. The builder, ignorant of the other visitors, was quite tickled by the prospect of becoming a secret father. In due time a daughter was born to provide another intriguing question for the village gossips.

About a year after this event, tragedy struck. The builder, who had always been a bit short of puff, expired at an ill-opportune moment during a visit to Edie. In her anxiety to telephone for the doctor from the box just across the road from her house, Edie, commendably, did not waste time clothing her person. Thus, old Newson, wending his way home from the Anchor, wondered if he had imbibed too heavily when a naked woman streaked across the road in front of him. By the time the doctor arrived Edie, intent on preserving the deceased's reputation, had made an effort to dress him. From the outset the doctor probably didn't believe Edie's story about the builder feeling ill and being invited to lie down on her bed to rest. He most certainly didn't on unbuttoning the deceased's shirt and finding a delicate article of Edie's underwear trapped under an armpit. Being a kindly man he made no comment other than to confirm heart failure.

Once the undertakers were involved the news and circumstances spread round the village as fast as a glass of old Newson's mangel wine goes to the head. Edie was surprisingly outspoken about her loss, remarking to a woman friend: 'It was a lovely way for him to go.' It could be said that the builder's sudden departure from this life put Edie on her feet, for in his will he left her the cottage and £5 a week for ten years for the welfare of the child – a sum quite sufficient to maintain all Edie's family in those days.

Soon after the bereavement the Second World War erupted. In

the ensuing war years Edie contributed to the war effort by entertaining the troops. But then the Americans arrived. Whether it was envy over the tinned foods, confectionery, silk stockings and cigarettes that Edie received in abundance – and happily shared with friends – or a genuine social concern for the good name of the village that caused action to be planned, I can but conjecture. Heavy G.I. traffic to and from Edie's house, to say nothing of jeeps parked overnight outside, led certain upper-crust ladies in the neighbourhood to approach the vicar. The vicar, who had long before given up any hope of persuading Edie to conform to the morals of the time, was loath to be involved and suggested to the ladies that if they felt so strongly that a house of ill repute had been established they should approach the law. The ladies, however, insisted that the vicar's stated disapproval was an essential pre-liminary to getting the police to act – no doubt they were mindful of the rumour that Edie's boy looked remarkably like the bobby. Much against his will, and only because he did not want to alienate the flower-arranging and church-assistance force the ladies composed, the vicar agreed to accompany Mrs Ludington-Witt on a cycling observation of the goings-on described to him.

Thus at around 9 o'clock one summer evening Mrs Ludington-Witt led the way as the two cycled down the road towards the house fronted by a parked jeep. So intent were they on trying to see what was happening behind Edie's windows that the vicar's front wheel rammed into Mrs Ludington-Witt's pedal. The collision resulted in both parties being thrown off. Mrs Ludington-Witt, a lady of ample proportions, landed on her back with the vicar on top of her in a most compromising position. In the confusion, Mrs Ludington-Witt apparently thought she had been assailed by a sex maniac G.I. and screamed 'Rape!' at the top of her voice. The vicar, trying not very successfully to disentangle himself, uttered a winded and pacifying 'No, no, Mrs Ludington-Witt, it's me' at which the shocked woman screeched even louder. Two Americans were soon on the scene to help the pair up and retrieve bicycles. Mrs Ludington-Witt was helped into Edie's cottage and given two double scotches to restore her composure. The vicar was likewise persuaded and then he and Mrs Ludington-Witt plus their cycles were jeeped home by their benefactors – who would probably not have been so keen had they known the original mission of those they befriended. The vicar, not used to hard liquor, found the sensation quite pleasurable and concluded that Edie Mortlake was not so bad after all if such was her hospitality. As for Mrs Ludington-Witt, her personal embarrassment was sufficient to make her drop the campaign against Edie.

Boosting Uncle Sam's morale proved to be costly for Edie – despite her expertise, she 'slipped up'. Jumping off the top of step ladders, soaking in hot baths and taking vile concoctions containing Epsom Salts failed to have the desired effect. Edie bore a third child.

A year or so after the war, Edie, faced with the ending of the builder's legacy payments and now with a larger family to support, looked for new security. Much to everyone's surprise, she married. The groom was a young steward in the Merchant Navy who seemed quite happy to take on a ready-made family. His periodic absence from home was a fortunate bonus for Edie, who did not seem to have any qualms about adultery, although her amorous liaisons did become less frequent. She also exhibited a new-found enthusiasm for the Women's Institute and other village social gatherings. One such was a weekly dance at the Village Hall where she took the entrance money and handed out tickets. Through this she met and began an affair with the accordion player in the band, a lean, lecherous Lothario some years her junior. With the key to the little used ante-room at the rear of the building in their possession, the lovers exchanged favours among the old carpets, stage props and drapes during the band's interval. Another member of the band, who did not much care for the accordionist, found out about the secret love-making and spitefully decided to make it public. One weekend, when the key to the ante-room was back on its hook in the lobby, he concealed the spare vocalist microphone under some drapes and ran a cable round the skirting and under the door to connect to the amplifying system. During the interval at the next dance, the Chairman of the Parish Council drew tickets for raffle prizes to a background of heavy breathing, giggles, moans and other mysterious sounds.

As the years passed Edie's amorous adventures featured less and less in local gossip. The title of village tart was usurped by younger rivals, although none had Edie's staying power. Her own children, it should be said, did not follow in mother's ways and her two daughters married young and lived conventional lives. Edie, however, was never without a man on the side up to the time her husband retired from the cross-Channel ferries.

Age brings many changes, not least the puzzling reversal of attitudes I mentioned earlier. One day not so long ago I went into the self-service store in the village street to make a purchase. There was Edie, neat, trim, and heavily made-up, gossiping with the woman at the payout desk. They were chatting in lowered tones but not low enough to prevent my hearing that the subject was the conduct of a local girl who had been living with one boy and had now moved in with another. I distinctly heard Edie observe: 'The way these young girls carry on nowadays is absolutely disgraceful.' It was not only what she said; she said it as if she meant it!

I Didn't Know Him
But I Dug His Grave

I hear that Charlie Gaybarrow is dead. For years he was the village gravedigger – he had been around so long that he had acquired an air of permanence. Over the span of half a century his appearance never seemed to change; he never looked any older and he always dressed in the same manner. Charlie Gaybarrow wasn't much of a socialiser; he never went in a pub and he spent most of his spare time in his garden. So when an old-time fellow villager was mentioned in conversation, Gaybarrow was likely to say, 'I didn't know him but I dug his grave.' In time this became a village catch phrase.

For one who must have turned a prodigious amount of soil in his time, Gaybarrow hardly had the physique one would associate with such strenuous work. Short and lithe and weighing no more than nine stone, he could nonetheless wield a spade – 'me scafel' he called it – with surprising agility. He could dig himself out of sight so rapidly that a mole would stand in awe. When I was a choirboy I often witnessed his labours, but I can recall him only as marking the turf or as lost from view in the grave, nothing in between.

As soon as he had completed his work Gaybarrow would allow himself the luxury of a pipe of baccy, settling down in the bottom of the grave to smoke it. This became something of a ritual and the sight of smoke wafting up from the ground signified Gaybarrow was having a well-earned breather. On one occasion one of the more cheeky choirboys crept across the graveyard and threw a large pine cone into the hole from which the familiar wisp of smoke was coming. Gaybarrow didn't have a nickname that I know of, but it should have been Lightning. The boy only had time to turn on his heels to run when Charlie leapt out of the hole, jumped several gravestones, boxed the boy's ears and disappeared from whence he came in less time than it takes to tell. No one ever tried that caper again.

About the biggest catastrophe that ever befell Gaybarrow was the time the vicar's sister stopped by to exchange a few words on the weather and unfortunately lost her footing and ended up right on top of the pipe-puffing Gaybarrow. Neither he nor the lady suffered any damage, although ribald pub rumour had it that his pipe set fire to her knickers and it took him rather a long time to make sure the fire was out!

There was considerable enmity between Gaybarrow and the vicar of my choirboy times. The vicar always appeared to be spying on Gaybarrow, who in turn always had a crafty eye cocked for the vicar. At the time I assumed that the vicar had probably got word of some of Gaybarrow's profitable sidelines. One was the sale of earthworms to juvenile fishermen. Threepence for a baccy tin of large ones and sixpence for small ones, with a penny back if you returned the tin. The transaction was never conducted at the graveside where the vicar might see, but in the small shed in the churchyard where Gaybarrow kept his sharpening tools and parked his bike. The gravedigger was a man of few words – at least I thought so then – and all you got on handing him your threepence was a terse: 'Bring the tin back. Don't say nothin' to the vicar.' After a while it became noticeable to us that the number of worms per tin had declined. When the supplier was challenged our complaints were brushed aside with: 'They's full when I fill em. 'Spect the big uns is eatin the little uns.'

It was about this time that word of Gaybarrow buying his own cottage from his landlord caused much speculation as to how he had got the money together. We choirboys quickly renamed his cottage 'Worm Hall' and its occupant 'Wormturd' – behind his back. Despite good business in the sale of bait, Gaybarrow's capital was more likely accumulated through his main occupation which was done on a piece work basis at so much per grave. The exact sum for each excavation he kept secret, although the price asked must have been highly competitive, for his services were also used by three other parishes in the district. The animosity that existed between Gaybarrow and our vicar was largely due to the vicar feeling that he was paying far too much in view of the speed with which each job was completed. He paid great attention to the size of each hole to ensure that he was getting his money's worth, an attitude that did not please Gaybarrow. Another source of Gaybarrow's income was assisting our local undertaker in various ways and, as I was eventually to discover, there was a great deal of collusion.

As I have said, Gaybarrow tended to keep himself very much to himself and as the years rolled by I never had more than the occasional opportunity to bid him good-day as he cycled by and received no more than a 'mornin'' or 'arternoon' in response. Thus I was surprised to discover one day that he was not always the reticent individual he seemed.

It must have been during a summer 25 to 30 years after my choirboy days. I was walking along the edge of a roadside field when I saw Gaybarrow coming in the distance. He was on his cycle, pedalling steadily, shoulders hunched over the handlebars, attired – or so it seemed – just as he had been in my boyhood: cloth cap pulled well down, faded fawn raincoat, collarless white shirt with stud at the neck, corduroy trousers folded and cycle-clipped above polished black boots. The precious scafel, as always, tied along the crossbar of the cycle, the blade protruding behind the saddle and wrapped round with a piece of tarpaulin to ensure that not a speck of rain should fall on the glistening steel. It was the same aged high-frame bike too, with the saddle stem cut down to compensate for the rider's lack of length in the leg. Before Gaybarrow reached me I noticed he kept looking down at his front wheel. Then, coming to a halt, he dismounted and appeared to be making an inspection of the wheel. When I drew level I called out a salutation and received the response: 'Puncture.'

I crossed into the road.

'Is it a bad one?' I enquired.

'Won't pump up. Have to mend it. Got me puncture outfit in me carrier box.'

I held the cycle while he untied the string bows that secured his scafel, removed it carefully and reverently laid it down among the toadflax on the road verge. This allowed him access to the lid of the carrier box, which he then opened. As he took out a neatly wrapped bundle containing the puncture outfit I noticed several well-worn tobacco tins. Worms, I thought; probably the same old tins . . . I suffered a pang of nostaglia.

'Gonna be a job. Front tyre's a stiff 'un to get off.'

'I'll give you a hand,' I said, turning the cycle upside down. He was right, the tyre was stiff and took some shifting. Like its owner it had seen many years. Gaybarrow held the bike while I struggled. I tried to make conversation and was surprised when his usual economy with words gave way to quite long and graphic accounts of the kind one usually associated with old Newson.

'You still digging graves?' I enquired.

'Just done a couple over Longham.'

'You've been at it a long while, haven't you?'

'Forty-four year come December.' And then after a pause he continued: 'Thas getting a bit too much now. I'm comin' up to 68. I'll still keep me hand in but I ain't gonna do all them other parishes.'

'Who'll take over?'

'You won't find any that'll do it by hand now. All done by machine. Use nothin' else at Ipswich 'cept in the old churchyards where the machines can't get. They'll soon use machines everywhere. Bloody mess they make too.'

'Oh?'

'Yes. There's more to it than just digging a hole yer know. Machine'll never do it like it can be done by hand. Like all things today, rough and ready.' There was a note of resigned despair in this utterance.

'Must be a monotonous job by hand,' I suggested.

'Ah, thas 'cause you don't know nothin' about it. You think each hole is the same. They ain't. Each is different. No sense in diggin' out more than's needed. Coffins look the same to ordinary people but they's all different. How come an undertaker make his money? He may charge the same price but you can be as sure as tomorrow he's measured up them that is goin' in and he won't use a half inch more wood than he has too. Same's with weight. If them that's goin' in is light then that'll be thin board that's used. 'course, thems that's payin' will get charged the same as if it were thick board. Thas like that with grave diggin. You go an see what size of coffin is agoin' in first. If the undertaker has cut down on the height or width then you don't have to take out so much dirt but you charge the same. I've saved myself a lot of sweat that way. Mind you, that old vicar we had here awhile back, I had some trouble with him. He was a tight old bugger. Always tryin' to knock me down on the price if he thought he weren't gettin' his moneysworth of hole. He'd come creepin' up as soon as I was done and measure up. Times he'd come along while I was just chucking the last spit out and drop a plumb-line down to see if it was six foot. Six foot I'm payin' yer for and not an inch less he'd say, the tight old sod. Ah, I got the better of him though. One day we were arguin' when the verger call out the vicar's wanted on the tele-

phone. Old fool left his plumb-line lying on the ground. As soon as he was out of sight I had me fingers over the edge of the grave to grab the line and when he come back it were six inches shorter. After that I'd dig about five foot seven and when he come round and plumbed the hole he'd think he was gettin' more than six foot. "That's a good man, spot on," he'd say, the old hippycrit. He'd go away thinking he'd got an inch for free. Best day's work I ever did was when he popped off and I had to dig his grave. You always wanted your money's worth – I said to myself – and now I'm going to give it you for free. I put that hole down another extra three feet I did. When the new vicar come along he says: "Thas a rather deep grave isn't it?"

' "Might be a little," I says, all innocent like. What I'd like to have said is: "Yes, that is deeper 'cause I thought I'd do him a kindness and see his nearer to where he's a goin'." '

Gaybarrow's face betrayed not a trace of humour. I liberated the tube from beneath the tyre, fascinated by the disclosures which I hoped would continue. They did.

'Cor, I had some trouble with that old man. Other vicars they leaves you to it, but he was always a nigglin'. Trouble was he weren't a practical man. Do you remember Draughty Dodds?'

I nodded.

'He were an enormous grut feller, weren't he? Got blown up by one of old Hitler's doodlebug bombs durin' the war. His was the biggest grave I ever did dig. Like a fool I set to afore I'd seen the undertaker. Blast man, when it come to it all they could find of Draughty after he were blown up weren't enough to fill a brown paper bag. So the undertaker made a small coffin and I dug a new hole. As for the first great hole I'd dug, I puts some boards across and the turf back tidy like. I knew we'd be wantin' a big one soon 'cause I'd seen that Mrs . . . can't remember her name, lived down against the school – perhaps you remember her? She were 18 stone I reckon . . . were lookin' a bit seedy and I knew she weren't goin' to last the winter. The old vicar he didn't like that. I didn't see nothin' wrong. Only common sense. I tell him there's a war on and we got to be economical.'

'Dyin's dyin' and it ain't no good pretendin' it ain't goin' to happen. Any gravedigger worth his salt 'll keep an eye out for who's likely to pop off during the winter and set himself up accordin'.'

'Oh? What do you mean?' I queried.

'Well, if there's a hard frost and the ground is frozen you can't make a good job apart from the fact you has a hell of a job to get started. So a good gravedigger will always cut turf and start a few as he think fit before the winter set in. Put the turf back carefully and that'll take an expert to see anything has been touched. Old vicar, he never did notice otherwise he'd have blew his top. Mind you a hard winter is always good for trade. Take '47, I had no end of work, people was poppin' off all over. You don't do no good when its mild.'

We finally mended the puncture and got the wheel inflated. Gaybarrow went on his way without so much as a thank you. Although I assumed that the ice had broken and that I would thereafter receive a more cordial salutation when we met, I still got no more than a 'Mornin' ' or 'Arternoon' as he went by.

Gaybarrow must have retired several years ago for it is now a long time since I've seen him pedalling by, scafel between his legs. He must have been a very old man when he died. Its sad to see one of the village characters go and even sadder in this case to think that his own grave will be dug by the long-haired young man operating the yellow JCB he despised so much. Still, I have an uncanny feeling that if you asked the long haired young man about Charlie Gaybarrow he would answer: 'I didn't know him but I dug his grave.'

Thoughts on Family Nicknames

Up to the middle of this century family nicknames were common in this district, a practice that now appears to have died out. Perhaps it had something to do with permanency, for at one time there were families who had been in the village for several generations, becoming very much a regular part of the scene. Now, since the development of modern communications, many have spread far and wide. Some, which were 30 or 40 strong, counting the various branches, are no longer to be found here at all.

The family nicknames were always a mystery to me for, with one exception which I will come to presently, no one has ever been able to tell me their origin. There were the 'Nibby Teggerts', 'Bramble Blakes', 'Pork Sparrows', 'Comey Smiths', and 'Briar Smiths', to name just a few. I once asked old Bramble Blake how he got that nickname. He fixed me with his one good eye – the other was glass – and indignantly replied: 'Thas a stupid thing to ask a feller!' As he was obviously annoyed I didn't press the question further; in any case, I'm sure he didn't know the answer.

I call them family nicknames because they were applied to several members and generations with confusing consequences. For example, the Briar Smith family – and there were at least six different strains of Smith in this parish alone – consisted of father and four boys, all known as Briar by the locals. It could be a trifle confusing unless one managed to elicit a Christian name as well. The nicknames were, of course, only used by others, never by the families concerned to identify themselves to other people.

In some cases there was delineation; the Honker Clarks for instance. There was Honker, his younger brother went as Young Honker and Young Honker's son was plain Honk. Young Honker's twin daughters were known simply as the Honker Gals. His eldest daughter was usually referred to, behind her back, by the quaint epithet 'River Bank'. The origin of this is known but the less said the better. The Honker Clarks are one of the families that have all moved away. I know the whereabouts only of Honker – that is Old Honker – who lives in one of the almshouses in a neighbouring village. He must be pushing 90, for many years have passed since his retirement from a lifelong stint of shepherd on one of the largest-acreage farms in the area. An old-type shepherd whose flock was his absorbing interest, Honker was rarely absent from his sheep.

Until the advent of modern dips, injections and feeding additives, sheep were not particularly popular with farmers around here; there were less troublesome ways of making a living. Indeed Honker's employer once confessed to my Guv'nor that his flock never made him any money and that the only reason he kept them was to keep Honker happy. Such a benevolent stance was hogwash, for this man was one of the most commercial farmers round about. Perhaps the flock did not pay as well as other enterprises, but his sheep would all have been mutton had the books failed to balance. As it was, he took great pride in his sheep and exhibited them – under Honker's watchful eye – at many county shows. Individual rams and ewes brought home several rosettes and now and again a cup. On more than one occasion a picture of the successful animal and Honker appeared in the farming papers. The wits in the Anchor professed great difficulty in distinguishing man from beast, finally deciding that the one with the hat must be Honker – all this deliberately in earshot of the shepherd when he was in the Anchor for a quick pint or to refuel his baccy pouch. Unperturbed, Honker dismissed such deliberations with a few choice words advising how difficult it would be to tell which end up any of his tormenters might be if they were photographed.

Honker, who was not easily intimidated, took such leg-pulling in his stride. A small man, not more than an inch over five feet, he presented a quite aggressive look. His angular face was surmounted by a cloth cap firmly pulled down so that the peak was almost on his eyebrows. I cannot recall ever seeing him without a cap, unless it was when he wore the trilby at county shows. Perhaps always being in the shade had preserved his eyesight for as far as I am aware he never wore glasses. Those bright, beady eyes could still read off the miniscule directions on a bottle of sheep dose by lantern light when he was near to retiring age.

Honker's wiry body belied a considerable strength. Not much bigger than some of his Suffolks, he still seemed to manhandle them with ease. When complimented on his ability to upend a ewe with one smart move, he would beam and say 'Thas all in the balance – like one of them ballet dancers.' Honker's supreme trick in the cause of moving a reluctant sheep from A to B involved approaching from the rear and somehow grasping the animal under its front legs to haul it up so that it was standing on its hind legs. Thus secured the sheep would be frog-marched, its back supported against Honker's front. Stepping out in unison the pair could move at quite a fast rate. It proved an unusual spectacle for the uninitiated. As can be expected, some of Honker's coarser compatriots, such as Old Rue and Wully, offered a crude explanation of what was really going on.

Like many countrymen, Honker preferred his own company and was not one for regular socialising or gossiping. He seemed never so contented as when he was tending his flock, seven days a week, night and day, off and on. At lambing time he would be in the field 24 hours a day, catching a wink or two of sleep in the shepherd's hut. Rather like a large chicken house on wheels, the structure bore a small maker's plate which fixed its date of construction as 1907. The better to improve its mobility, just after the Hitler war, Honker's employer had the original cast-iron wheels removed and pneumatic tyres off some scrapped army vehicle fitted in their place. At the same time, as the hut had no steerage, a fixed drawbar was fitted to one end so this could be hitched to and lifted up by one of the then new little grey Ferguson tractors and the hut easily conveyed from field to field. Previously it had to be laboriously manhandled onto a trailer for movement along the road. Further renovation included the installation of a window in one side and a bunk bed over the cupboard where the sheep medicines were kept. The interior was fairly spartan, the only furniture being a backless chair, rough table-cum-shelf under the window and a battered armchair. I could not hazard a guess at the original colour of the armchair as it was so faded, stained and hung with particles of greasy wool as to be beyond identification. Few visitors ventured into the shepherd's hut, for the simple reason that the smell therein was vile. Sheep, medicines and tobacco were undoubtedly the main elements of the pong; it was not the sort you lingered with in order to define. Honker was undoubtedly conditioned to it and unaware of its obnoxious quality.

The interior of the hut contrasted dramatically with that of Honker's cottage. There everything was spotless and shining. Mrs Clark was houseproud and she held sway with similar care in the garden, where never a weed was to be seen. Her industry was commendable, but, sadly, it was not for this that she was renowned among the village folk, but for her extraordinary meanness. This was not because of poverty; Honker was better paid than the foreman on his farm and Mrs Clark earned a regular and useful sum for 'doing' at the chapel and the village hall. The Clarks had no family of their own. Wully observed cruelly and crudely: 'If she don't ever open that tight fist of hers, you can be sure she weren't ever going to open her legs!' A more plausible reason would be Honker's absence from the marriage bed, for he was rarely at home. Moreover his pipe was not tolerated in the dwelling and his drinking habits not approved of. Honker was not normally a pub drinker; an odd pint yes, but mostly he imbibed on his own during sheepwatch. One of his treasured possessions was an ornate hip flask given him by the officer whose horse he groomed during his service in the First World War. The contents of this flask may occasionally have been whisky or brandy when accumulated pocket money ran to this, or if his employer presented a bottle for services rendered. More often it was wild home-distilled spirit acquired from old Newson, who was his cousin. Whatever the nature of the contents, the hip flask was rarely absent from the old army greatcoat Honker regularly wore for the best part of the year. If not in the pocket, it was in hand for what Honker referred to as 'A little nip'. Considering the foul weather he had to face in ministering to his flock, the frequent nips were justified. Often they must have been very frequent for, although I never heard of him drunk, at times he did get very merry. You could always tell when he had really indulged himself because then he tended to talk to the sheep. On several occasions I have passed his sheep folds at night and heard soothing words coming from the vicinity of the old gas lamp he used as he tended some poorly animal.

While general opinion in the village held that Honker was dominated by his wife and a pretty mild-mannered fellow, if matters really got out of hand he could display a considerable temper to match his fierce looks. I witnessed an example of this one day when a ewe he was doctoring stamped on his already sore foot. The flow of invective would have done any sergeant major proud – to say nothing of horrifying his Chapel-going wife had she been in earshot. Honker's anger was terrible to see. The storm was brief and his usual placid mood soon returned.

Honker was plying his skills long before I came on the scene, so at a rough guess his shepherding must have lasted 40–45 years. There are many anecdotes told about him and before I get to one that has a connection with family nicknames, let me relate one from a few years earlier.

Early in 1949 or a year thereabouts, when he was in his early fifties, Honker was the victim of an audacious prank. One slightly foggy evening four local lads walking to the pub for a drink passed the meadow where Honker's flock was lambing. Through the mist the lantern light could be seen and comforting words heard, the latter suggesting that Honker had been at the 'little nips'. Passing the dark shape of the shepherd's hut close by the road hedge at one corner of the meadow, the lads agreed on a mischievous deed. They quietly slipped over the gate and approached the hut. They lifted up the steps to the door and placed them inside, together with the wood chocks from the wheels. Next, they heaved against the hut, which moved surprisingly easily over the turf. The width of the field against the road was probably no more than a couple of hundred yards and on reaching the far corner the steps were repositioned and the wheels chocked, leaving the hut more or less as it was – apart from the different location. This was all accomplished in silence. The four tricksters fled the scene in haste as they saw Honker's lamp coming near. Hiding in a ditch they watched the light reach the corner where the hut had stood. It remained stationary for a while and then moved in a zig-zag fashion. Faint mumbling was audible, though no words could be distinguished. After a few minutes the light moved along the road hedge to the accompaniment of more mumbling. An erratic course finally brought the light to the repositioned hut. The mumbling ceased and the door closed on the light. The four lads continued on to the pub, speculating on Honker being so 'nipped' that he was unaware that the hut had been moved and believed that his drink-befuddled mind had taken him to the wrong side of the field. The plan was to repeat the exercise on the way home. In the event it required a half hour wait until the light emerged from the hut and moved off down the field. Again the shelter was quietly pushed along to more or less where it had originally reposed earlier that evening. As the hour was late and the lads were cold they did not wait to see the results. I know all this because, to my shame, I was one of them.

In the days that followed, as there were no reports of Honker giving voice to strange happenings in the night, it was assumed that he had indeed been too happy to appreciate the movements of his hut. We were wrong, as a glance over the hedge revealed when I next passed the lambing meadow. The steel pin driven into the ground beside a wheel and a chain shackled round it provided evidence that the shepherd was well aware that there had been goings on.

A shepherd's life in those days was still a lonely one and the work provided little excitement. Yet Honker managed to be involved in the odd incident that provided much mirth for others if not for him. The supreme occasion, which will long be a favourite yarn for relating in the snug at the Anchor or the Lamb, concerns a harvest festival in a neighbouring village church. In the forceful language heard in the pubs it is referred to as the 'Famous Bugger-up'. In the drawing rooms of local gentlefolk it is known as 'That Infamous Fiasco'. The whole affair was like something out of a West End theatre farce. Honker played the star role.

To begin at the beginning, one has to understand the competition that used to exist between the custodians of holy places. Just as pubs gain and wane in popularity, so did places of worship. Just as a jovial landlord or a nubile barmaid can pile them into the public bar, so could an eloquent and showman vicar fill the church pews. During the Fifties there were several such clergymen in this district. One, the encumbent of a neighbouring village, was particularly competitive. At Harvest Festival time his church was by far the best decorated in the county. One year he decided to go beyond the usual fruit, vegetables, flowers and farm implements and have real livestock. After some discussion at the Parochial Church Council this was narrowed down to 'safe' creatures, namely bantams, rabbits and sheep. Honker's employer, a member of this Council, was persuaded, or volunteered, to provide four placid ewes. He assumed that they would be penned in the churchyard, but the ambitious parson had other ideas and arranged for a pen of wooden hurdles to be erected inside the church near the font. At first Honker did not take kindly to his employer's news and told him so. Being strictly Chapel, even though he never went near the place, he protested it was against his religious principles. Eventually, after it was pointed out as also being an opportunity to show off two of his prizewinning animals, Honker's attitude changed, although he still feigned disapproval.

Arrangements were made for the sheep to be delivered to the church on the Sunday morning preceding the Harvest Festival service and for their removal on the following Monday morning. A couple of old tarpaulins were laid on a ground base on the church floor and capped with a liberal dressing of straw. Hurdles were erected and bound one to another with baler wire. A structure for holding hay was placed in the centre of the pen as was a water trough. Honker having approved the accommodation, the sheep were transported by tractor and trailer to be ushered into their new accommodation with little difficulty.

All four ewes demonstrated unusual docility considering they were the centre of attraction and rarely free from adult gaze and the exclamations of children. Honker, who didn't really trust church-going folk, made the bar of the Wheelwright's Arms across the road from the church gate, his headquarters, tracking back and forth to keep an eye on things. Following a splashing experience the vicar decided bales of straw should be placed outside the hurdles to prevent similar misfortune befalling worshippers. At the same time the baling wire on the hurdles was replaced with strong red tape which the vicar felt had more aesthetic appeal.

For the grand Sunday morning service Honker was present in his country show suit and trilby. Mrs Clark had at some time attempted to launder the suit with the result that it had shrunk severely, the jacket only just buttoning across Honker's modest figure. Otherwise, given that the suit was only donned once or twice a year, its condition was good for its age.

The church filled to capacity, with a large body of people having to stand at the back. Much to Honker's annoyance, several standing families positioned themselves between his location and the sheep pen so that at times he could less easily keep a beady eye on his woolly charges. Nevertheless all went well until the last verse of the final hymn.

In tying his nice big red bows round the hurdles, the vicar had not allowed for a bored and fiddly small boy. To youngsters, bows are for pulling. Honker, who had been respectfully following the lead of those round about in kneeling, standing and sitting, was suddenly confronted with the sight of a ewe's rear end departing down a side aisle. Instead of trying to contain the animals, men, women and children had moved smartly aside. 'They 'ont hurt yer,' bawled Honker, to no avail as all four occupants of the fold were now running free. The leading ewe was confronted by a sidesman with a collecting plate. This stout fellow held his ground while other members of the congregation rose from their seats and attempted to 'shoo' the sheep back. Before retreating the animal, as is often the result of fright, deposited an offering. This was not what the sidesman wanted, or apparently noticed, for a moment later he had stepped in it and was so disturbed that he dropped the collecting plate. A considerable part of the congregation on that side of the church crawled on hands and knees to pick up the scattered coins, maybe – at first – unaware of the ewe's parting gesture. There is no need to dwell further on the outcome other than to say that some people became more immersed in an agricultural experience than they had bargained for.

Meanwhile the sheep were being pursued in other parts of the nave. At one point a ewe tried to escape between two occupied pews which had several ladies standing on their seats screaming. The vicar, having hastily brought the service to a close, stood bemused in the chancel.

Honker, having managed to get one ewe back in the fold, made haste after a prize animal heading towards the chancel. He finally overtook it in the front of the nave below the pulpit. Instead of driving the animal back, the exhibitionist in Honker asserted itself and he attempted one of his renowned frog-marching acts. The polished wood block floor did not offer the same boot security as a meadow, however, and as he attempted to up-end the ewe Honker's legs slid from under. As a result he ended up on his back with the kicking ewe on top of him. The four occupants of the front pew looked on incredulously at this grappling heap of man and sheep. As his own efforts to rise seemed to be getting him nowhere, Honker fixed his eye on Brigadier Venables, occupying the end seat, and demanded: 'Don't just bloody sit there a-garpin'. Git hold of its legs'. The brigadier obeyed, finally managing to grab a kicking back leg. Unfortunately the ewe had more strength than the old brigadier; it threw him across the laps of three ladies.

None of the ladies uttered a word or made a movement at this unexpected development. That is, until the old gentleman attempted to raise himself. Unbeknown to the brigadier his tie clasp had become snagged in Mrs Cynthia Aidswell's hand-knitted wool dress and when the old boy tried to get up the lady found her skirt going too. In her alarm she took the only immediate action possible, pulling him down again. The brigadier had knocked around and taken a tumble or two in his time and he was not for pinning down by some Anglican matron. 'Let go,' he barked, only to be hauled down again as Mrs Aidswell felt her dress leaving her ample thighs. With this peculiar scrummage going on right before his eyes no wonder the vicar was struck dumb. The brigadier's foggy brain finally picked up Mrs Aidswell's pleas of 'You're caught on my dress,' and this little contretemps sorted itself out. By then Honker had finally got the better of the ewe and frog-marched it back up the main aisle in triumphant fashion. His trilby remained firmly in place.

In an inspired effort to be helpful the verger opened the church door while the congregation drove forth the two sheep still at liberty and flooded out after them. 'We'll never catch the . . . . . . s – them – now' protested Honker, calming down sufficiently to remember his language. Fortunately several of his old acquaintances were assembled outside the Wheelright's Arms awaiting a different kind of service. Honker was able to enlist their help to finally catch and secure the errant sheep. During this operation the vicar, who evidently felt he was partly responsible for their escape, walked up and down the road outside the church murmuring: 'Oh dearie me, oh dearie me, oh dearie me.' These repeated utterances did not go unnoticed by the patrons of the Wheelright's Arms. Often to be heard in the public bar during the weeks to come was the mocking chant of 'Oh dearie me, oh dearie me.'

Honker insisted the experience so frightened the ewes involved that they were almost a write-off. 'Do you see, they'll never stand for the ram again and dare say their wool 'on't be no good,' he moaned. His fears were in fact unfounded, but the whole episode reinforced Honker's contempt for churchgoers. 'Thas would nev-er have happened in chapel,' he said. 'They folks know how to tie a proper slip knot. They church lot can't even keep their own boot laccs tight!'

The fiasco evidently did no harm to the ambitious vicar's reputation with the church hierarchy. The last I heard of him he had made bishop in a northern city. Before the move he spent a few more years as a local parson and became generally known – behind his back – as 'Oh dearie mc' or 'The Reverend Oh dearie me'. His wife became 'Mrs Oh dearie me', his eldest daughter 'The Gal Oh dearie me', and his younger daughter 'Little Oh dearie me'. This younger girl suffered a change of nickname when it became known that an unfortunate association with a hippie evangelist had led to an embarrassing pregnancy. She then became known as 'Pudden'd Oh dearie me'. This is the only family nickname for which I know the origin. For that matter it was the last I heard of around here. Mind you, from what old Newson has said I have a suspicion that one may have been bestowed on our family. Sometimes ignorance is bliss.

Comey Smith's Lurcher

I haven't a lot of time for dogs. They may be best friend to many a human but I've always found them smelly, hair-shedding, road-fouling animals inclined to bite or lick one as the fancy takes them. I will admit that there are some real characters among them. Old Newson's mongrel regularly fetched his daily paper from the front gate and the village grocer's Pekinese would sit up in a begging position outside the butcher's shop. The one dog the Guv'nor had was a character too. It hated the local bobby. It would lie in wait until he came pedalling by and then pounce out and try and bite his leg. This caused the Guv'nor considerable embarrassment and often half a dozen eggs to placate the law.

It has been my misfortune to encounter many canine creatures over the years and of these, there is no doubt, the most extraordinary was Comey Smith's lurcher. There was nothing extraordinary about its looks; more light brown greyhound than collie. What singled this dog out was its behaviour – an artful villainy that made it infamous.

Perhaps this was only to be expected considering the dog's background. Comey Smith bought it as a puppy soon after he came out of the army. The vendor was Nasty, the animal being the progeny of his bitch, the epitome of a poacher's hound. With Nasty's reputation for dicey deals one can be sure he came best out of the transaction. Exactly how the deal was struck or if it involved the exchange of money, I know not. Comey Smith seemed well satisfied, having been informed by Nasty that the pup was a 'pedigree lurcher'. Comey Smith's father – Old Comey Smith – was less enthusiastic about his son's acquisition, probably because of the source; 'That'll be nothin' but trouble, do you see. That'll have the distempers and never rustle out a rabbit. Fool had better bought a blind ferret.'

The old boy was right about the trouble and wrong about the distemper and the inability to hunt. In fact, once matured, the lurcher displayed an uncanny ability to pick up rabbits and birds. Comey Smith liked to do a spot of poaching but wasn't renowned for his energy and never took the trouble to train the dog in the art of hunt and snatch. Rather it appears to have been a matter of genes, the lurcher's inherent qualities stemming from a long line of poaching forebears. One extraordinary aspect was the way that it retrieved – and of its own volition. Comey would take the dog down a lane and set it loose and within five minutes it would have picked up a rabbit or pheasant and brought it back to its master. At first Comey couldn't believe his luck. No scrambling through hedges and ditches and keeping one's head down to avoid game-keepers. The dog was a natural poacher, stalking its prey with cunning and avoiding any humans that might be in the vicinity.

It transpired that having tasted the joys of the chase over a period of several months, the lurcher became less inclined to return to the leash. This enraged Comey, who being a portly fellow was equally disinclined to run around trying to catch the animal. Neither did the dog continue to tolerate being chained up in the back garden shed, discovering that if a continual whining was kept up, the exasperated Comey would come out and set it free. His irritation at this show of defiance by the lurcher provoked much cursing about that 'f'in' dog'. Up to that time the animal had no given name, simply being called the pup or the dog. As a result of her husband's frequent references to the 'f'in' dog', Mrs Smith got into the habit of calling it 'F'. A neighbour assumed this was short for Effie and Mrs Smith, not liking to explain the true origin, concurred. The name stuck and no one seemed to question why such an effeminate tag as Effie was applied to a male.

Now rarely secured, the lurcher was off on its own for most of the day. Comey was agreeably surprised to find a rabbit deposited on his back doorstep when returning from his carpentry work one evening. He was even more pleased when a large cock pheasant turned up as an offering on the same altar. Indeed, as the weeks went by a regular supply of catches appeared, mostly rabbit and game bird which were quite suitable and welcome for the pot. Thus Comey was absolved from the effort of poaching while still receiving the rewards; a situation which suited him admirably, being disinclined to unnecessary exercise. However, he was a little uneasy when the bag included a couple of Mrs Maggs's guinea fowl and someone's tomcat.

Unfortunately, if not busy hunting, the lurcher was engaged in other activities around the neighbourhood which began to make it most unpopular. It was caught scraping out a large hole in the middle of Brigadier Venables's newly levelled and seeded lawn, but was gone before the old gentleman could fetch his shotgun. Even more damning, the lurcher started to use driveways into the new housing estate for lavatorial purposes, as several householders only discovered when they got indoors. Effie also lived up to the origin of his name by seemingly being present to mate with every bitch for miles around when nature called. He seems to have had most of his successes in the village street judging by the complaints. Once this exhibitionist and Fulger's spaniel bitch performed in front of the Sunday School outing party which was waiting for a coach to arrive. The embarassed vicar and his lady helpers tried to ignore the spectacle while the children found it all most entertaining. In fact, that evening, one little girl, when asked what she enjoyed most on the outing, launched into a rapturous description of the two doggies' antics to horrified parents. The vicar had a word with the policeman who in turn had a word with Comey about keeping the dog chained up.

The lurcher was not to be caught by coaxing words or bowls of food, being smartly off when anyone extended a hand its way. The canine menace stayed free. Of course, while it continued to bring back the occasional bunny and bird Comey was loath to secure it, despite the growing disquiet in the village over its other activities and habits. Besides, he didn't even have to provide food, the lurcher appeared to be securing its own meals.

The worn assertion that dogs are like their owners came to apply to the lurcher in that it often didn't trouble to go poaching having found an easier means of obtaining a meal. In those days the Co-op butcher's van travelled round the village twice a week. This had a display of meats and poultry behind large sliding side windows, enabling customers to select their requirements and instruct the butcher on what they wanted. When the van was parked outside the council houses one day, and while the butcher was waiting for his customers to come out, he saw the lurcher lurking nearby and threw it a scrap of offal. He made the mistake of doing this on several occasions, only to find the lurcher was regularly in attendance, following his van round the village. Matters came to a head when, while the butcher's back was turned and the serving window was open, the lurcher jumped up and made off with a string of sausages. Thereafter the butcher kept a small pile of stones in the van with which to drive off the regular nuisance. Not that he ever obtained a hit, for the dog was far too agile.

Intent on ridding himself of the lurcher's attentions he went so far as to acquire some rotten eggs, thinking that the splash effect might be more successful. Stepping out of the van's rear door to launch one of these missiles, he foolishly did not check the road behind him. The lurcher sped across the road, the egg following, only to burst on the front wheel of Edie Mortlake's bicycle. Edie was not her usual amicable self and without waiting for an explanation told the butcher what he could do with his pork chops and his 'divi'. This incident only increased the butcher's dislike of the lurcher and he plotted all sorts of horrible means to eliminate his tormenter.

Exhibiting surprising intelligence, Effie the lurcher began to transfer its interest from the butcher to the customer. The first known indication of the new trend occurred when the dog was caught trying to lift a joint off the kitchen table at Lane Farm just after the butcher had called. It had better luck at Obanwick House, home of Mr Pepperwell, a retired headmaster. A bachelor, he organised his daily routine almost as precisely as classroom lessons. On Wednesdays he always bought two lamb cutlets from the Co-op van, on Saturdays a small joint of beef – acquisitions that did not go unnoticed by Comey Smith's lurcher. Wednesday mornings also happened to be the regular spot for Alice Keswick, who also 'did' for my mother, to come for three hours' cleaning and sundry other chores at Obanwick House.

The retired schoolmaster was an able cook, but being of frugal disposition was disinclined to dispose of left-overs. These often reposed in his larder for many days, producing a rather unpleasant atmosphere therein. On her visits, one of the first things Mrs Keswick did was to open the pantry window to improve the air. She rarely succeeded in persuading her employer to dispose of any foodstuff unless it was actually going bad. Thus on Wednesdays when cutlets were carried up the garden path to be placed in the pantry meat safe at Obanwick House, the lurcher discovered an open invitation. An easy leap took it into the pantry where the scent of raw meat drew the dog to the safe standing on the floor. No doubt a sniffing investigation of the ill-fitting perforated-metal door also found that the push-pull catch was weak. Little effort was needed to paw the door open and the cutlets were liberated!

Not until going to retrieve the cutlets for his Thursday lunch did Pepperwell find the plate bare. He was mystified; for there were no clues to the thief – the safe door having swung shut and the pantry window having been closed by the charlady before leaving. The more he thought about it, the more he suspected Mrs Keswick. By the time the next Wednesday came round he had all but convinced himself of her guilt, deciding to keep her under surveillance during the morning domestics. Again his favourite cut was obtained from the Co-op butcher and placed in the meat safe. Again the lurcher quietly slipped in through the open pantry window and retrieved the meat for its own consumption elsewhere. Having spied on Mrs Keswick and noted that she only went into the pantry to open the window when she arrived and later on to shut it, on finding the cutlets had again disappeared Pepperwell had no doubt that she had quietly pocketed them.

A rational review of the circumstances would have shown that his 'help' would have been hardly likely to carry out such an obvious theft and a tactful approach to her about the missing cutlets might have quickly resolved the whole matter. Instead, the old fellow brooded on this business and was quite determined he would eventually catch Mrs Keswick, cutlet in hand, sneaking out of his pantry.

Pepperwell was in a rare old state by the following Wednesday. Once more he made his usual purchase from the Co-op van and placed it in his meat safe. He then kept a shifty eye on his employee as she dusted and polished, even hiding behind the long curtains of the hallway french window ready to apprehend the pantry robber. But on this Wednesday it was raining, perhaps not cats and dogs, but hard enough to deter Mrs Keswick from the usual ritual of opening the pantry window. In consequence she didn't go near the place and her employer was almost disappointed to find the meat still in the safe after her depature. Anyone less obsessed might have recognised the significance of the unopened window. Instead, the man brooded on, his one ambition to expose Mrs Keswick as the thief.

On her next visit the sun was shining and she swung wide the pantry window to clear the smell of a four-day-old, half-consumed onion pie. The pong was no deterrent to the artful lurcher, who wasted little time in making another successful raid once the meat was in the safe and the pantry door closed. Pepperwell watched and waited and come the time Mrs Keswick usually departed had tucked himself behind the french window curtains. When 'the help' tripped into the pantry to close the window he believed he had his thief. As she came out into the hallway Pepperwell made his move to bar her way and demand she empty her pockets. Such was his state of tension that he tripped over the bottom of the curtain and toppled over onto his suspect. Both went down for a none-too-soft landing on the parquet floor.

Now Alice Keswick was not unaware of Pepperwell's hovering and skulking about the house during this and the past two Wednesdays. While he was convincing himself she was a thief, Keswick was suspecting that Pepperwell had designs on her person. She interpreted Pepperwell's fall as an assault and defended herself with vigour. Smart action with a knee left Pepperwell wincing in agony. Scrambling to her feet Mrs Keswick grabbed the nearest thing to hand, a framed photograph of W.G. Grace hanging on the wall, to deal him a hefty blow to his bald pate before running for the door. When the battered Pepperwell finally struggled to his feet he dialled 999. The police arrived in force to discover the poor man smarting under a sizeable bump. It did not take them long to find sufficient evidence establishing how the cutlet thief had come and gone. From the paw marks in the flower bed our local bobby had a very good idea as to what was the culprit, particularly as Mrs Keswick later said she had seen the dog in Obanwick House garden that day.

The gist of what had happened reached Comey Smith before the policeman, giving him sufficient time to dream up a story that he had sold the lurcher to a man he met in a pub; the animal was no longer his responsibility. The bobby was not that easily taken in and read the riot act to the protesting Comey. The whole affair provided Alice Keswick, the village's prime gossip, with verbal ammunition to bore her various employers silly for years to come. She never 'did' for Pepperwell again.

Even Comey was becoming disenchanted with his wayward lurcher, and after its next piece of thieving, completely so. Having once discovered that kitchens contained appetising delicacies, Effie took a new interest in human habitation, particularly when a window or door was left open. At Edie Mortlake's one day Effie found on the kitchen dresser, among the clutter, a freshly gutted rabbit, no doubt a present from one of Edie's admirers. The lurcher started to devour the rabbit carcass. Hearing noises Edie came tripping downstairs. Surprised, the lurcher jumped down, then went back for the rabbit. In its haste it made off with Edie's cossack-style fur hat.

Finding what it had stolen uneatable, the lurcher left it on Comey's doorstep. Unfortunately, Mrs Comey Smith recognised the fur hat immediately and well aware of Edie's reputation, jumped to the wrong conclusion. A highly strung woman, Comey's missus had worked herself up into a considerable rage by the time her husband came in from work. A pail of cold water right over the head is not the most pleasant of greetings. The resulting fracas was eventually resolved after providing some entertainment for the neighbours. Having experienced the unfounded jealousy of his wife, the unlucky Comey then got an earful from Edie Mortlake about his thieving dog.

Worse was to come. The vicar's children had a white angora rabbit called Belinda that lived in a hutch at the back of the vicarage garden. This bunny was of venerable age, having been given to the children when they were quite small. One day the vicar came out of his house in time to see the lurcher investigating the rabbit hutch. A shout saw Effie depart in a hurry. Alas, too late, for while the rabbit had not been physically harmed, it had expired through shock. The vicar intended to make strong representations to the bobby that something be done about this accursed mongrel – he had not forgotten its performance in front of the Sunday School a couple of years previously. But first Charlie Gaybarrow was summoned from his normal graveyard tasks to dig a small hole beside the lychgate wall in which Belinda could be interred with all reverence. The service completed, the vicar and family in attendance, Gaybarrow returned to cover the deceased.

Gaybarrow was back in the grave he was digging on the far side of the churchyard, when he happened to look out and saw Comey Smith's lurcher making off at great haste with something off-white in its mouth. He quickly realised this was Belinda's corpse; the grave had been robbed! While Gaybarrow may not have liked the vicar, he disliked the lurcher even more. He had not forgotten the time when, being deep in one of his excavations, the dog had come by and cocked a leg against a fork left on the top. He hastened to the vicarage to report the grave-robbing. The vicar was beside himself with rage. After visiting the site of the crime he demanded that Gaybarrow be a witness when he confronted Comey Smith. Normally the gravedigger was not for giving the vicar any sort of support, but as he didn't like Comey Smith and given the opportunity would have happily buried his lurcher, he agreed.

Such was the vicar's preoccupation with the body snatching that he did not notice the amount of graveyard deposited on the floor and passenger seat of his precious Morris Minor by Gaybarrow's muddy boots and overalls. The vicar's driving usually left much to be desired in respect of safety; on this occasion it caused Gaybarrow to fear that somebody might shortly be digging both their graves. The good Lord looks after his own, for, after near misses with the District Nurse and a careless cat, the car screeched to a halt outside Comey Smith's cottage.

As it was a Saturday the vicar hoped to find Comey at home, but the door was opened by his wife. Unfortunately the vicar had worked himself up into such a state that he did not notice his own slip of the tongue in his opening blast. Mrs Smith, still not completely satisfied about the incident involving Edie Mortlake's fur hat, took it literally. The dialogue that transpired is as reported by Gaybarrow.

Vicar: 'You've got to do something about your letcher!'

Mrs Comey: 'Oh dear.'

Vicar: 'He's an absolute disgrace!'

Mrs Comey: 'Oh dear . . . was it Edie . . . ?'

Vicar: 'Belinda; he's got our Belinda. Frightened her to death.'

Mrs Comey: 'Oh dear. I don't know what's got into him lately.'

Vicar: 'She was at rest and he dragged her off into the bushes. It's a mercy my children didn't see it.'

Mrs Comey: 'Well, I don't know what to say. I never thought he was interested in . . .'

Vicar: 'He's a menace all over the village thieving – and there isn't a bitch that's safe.'

Mrs Comey (in tears): 'Oh no . . .'

Vicar: 'You'll have to have him chained up or otherwise he'll have to be put down.'

Mrs Comey: 'But Vicar!'

Vicar: 'I'm sorry to upset you but you'll have to tell your husband I'm reporting this to the police.'

Mrs Comey: 'You sure you haven't made a mistake?'

Vicar: 'No. I'd know that dog anywhere – Mr. Gaybarrow saw him do it – didn't you?'

Mrs Comey: 'But Vicar, you said . . .'

Here Charlie Gaybarrow interjected to tell the vicar what he had said. The vicar said he didn't. Mrs Comey said he definitely did and a man in his position should know better.

While this little misunderstanding was sorted out, Comey Smith had come out of the pub up the road after his Saturday mid-day pint. Seeing his wife and the vicar in what appeared to be an altercation, Comey decided the prudent thing to do was to go back into the pub for another pint. In fact his apprehension led him to have three more. When he did eventually return home even this alcoholic fortification failed to provide protection from his wife's wrath or from her ultimatum: either that dog goes or I do.

Comey, who liked a quiet life, the more so as time passed, had now finally turned against the lurcher. He tried to get Rue Scrutts to shoot it but the dog seemed to sense danger and kept well out of the way of the ambush that was set up. Comey also considered poisoning and other means of extermination. But all this planning proved unnecessary; fortune took a hand in events.

On the Saturday after the grave-robbing incident, the Women's Institute had its annual outing. Riddlestone's Luxury Coach picked up parties of ladies at various arranged stopping places in the village. When the coach stopped to pick up four old dears at Brick Lane Corner, the dreaded lurcher appeared out of the adjacent roadside hedge to investigate a stimulating odour coming from the opened luggage compartment at the rear of the coach. The local butcher's wife had supplied three dozen freshly cooked meat pies as a part of the midday fare for the outing. After the coach driver had put a couple of baskets in the back and gone around the side of the coach to help another lady on board, the lurcher moved in for a quick grab. But on this occasion it was not quite quick enough; for while it was still trying to find a way into the hamper holding the pies, the compartment door was slammed shut on it. The driver, finding no further items to stow, had hurriedly closed the compartment without noticing the prospecting thief.

Thus Riddlestone's Luxury Coach departed with Ernie Riddlestone at the wheel, 36 jolly W.I. passengers and a reluctant stowaway in the luggage compartment. Luxury may mean different things to different people, but it would be hard to find a definition of it that would encompass the standard of the suspension on that vehicle. The passenger seating may have afforded some dampening effect but the interior of the luggage hold magnified every jolt and jar. Even the remarkable constitution of the lurcher was no match for this so by the time the coach reached its destination, Whipsnade Zoo, some of the contents of the luggage compartment were less desirable than when first placed there. When Ernie Riddlestone lifted the compartment door he was more than a little taken aback when the lurcher shot out like a bullet and he surveyed the mess it had made. Suffice to say that apart from having to buy refreshments, the ladies all had a thoroughly enjoyable time that sunny day. The lurcher was not seen again. No doubt in this new life it was more than able to take care of itself.

When word reached Comey Smith of Effie's exit he could hardly believe his luck. Surely a distance of 108 miles was too great for the lurcher to find its way back. Probably as a form of consolation he was given to speculating that it had been eaten by a lion. Nevertheless, I think he has ever since lived in dread of finding a rabbit corpse on his back door-step.

The Itch

It was a hot, prickly sort of day and I was trying to dismantle an electric starter motor on the workshop bench. The wretched thing would not come apart at the right place and, frustrated, I was standing there, idly scratching my back with a screwdriver and pondering the next move, when a familiar voice called: 'Tryin' to find a loose screw?'

Old Newson was framed in the doorway, for once without his overcoat; it really must have been a hot day.

'No,' I laughed, 'Just scratching.'

'What, you got the itch then?' He came into the workshop, backed his bottom against the wall ledge, spread his feet and leaned forward on his walking stick. The signs were ominous.

'No, not really.' I sensed one of his outrageous yarns was about to be delivered and I really didn't want to be involved when I was busy. But, as usual, there was no escape.

'Just wondered if the old itch had shown up again. Expect it will one day.' He set the bait and I, foolishly, didn't recognise it.

'What itch is that?' I queried.

'You mean to tell me you bin around here all these years and you don't know nothin' about the itch? I thought as how you might have been one that has had it.'

'No, I don't know what you're on about.' I was hooked now.

'Well, perhaps you was too young when that first got around here but I thought you'd know all about it.' He repositioned his bottom on the ledge and made himself more comfortable. He was about to deliver.

'Tha's time the people who use to farm at Crow Hall grew greens for the London market. They had an old lorry and use to take a load of Brussels or cabbage up to Covent Garden most nights – London people is partial to them gassy old greens, they sit about so much their old guts need a bit of stirrin' up. Anyways, there weren't many lorries around here in them days – reckon that was about 1931 – no that were '32, time as Ind Coope bought the Anchor and you couldn't get brown bitter no more. Anyways, as I was sayin', there weren't many lorries around here then, so some of the lads in the village would go along just for the ride. Well, o'course they was bound to get up to no good. That London's a dirty place; ain't fit for God-fearin', clean livin' country people to go there. Well, one of the lads who use to go was . . . it ain't fair to mention his name; all I'll say is that he had ginger hair and once worked for your father and popped off about ten year ago; but it ain't fair to say who he were.'

I nodded in agreement, for I knew who he meant.

'Anyways, this lad worked for old Fenney the builder – you know, him that died on the nest round Edie Mortlake's – and one day old Fenney say to him: "Boy, I been a watching you lately; seems as I'll have to halve your wages as only one of your hands is working for me while the other is always a scratchin' your crotch."

The lad say: "I got a bad itch, Mr Fenney."

"Well," say Fenney, "do you go see Doctor Gates about it tonight." The lad were a bit nervous about going but come the weekend he found out from three of his mates what had been to Covent Garden that they was a scratchin' away like mad too. So they plucked up courage to go down the surgery together. "We got an itch," they say to Doctor Gates. Well, he has a look and knows right away what they been up to. He thinks to himself I'll teach 'em a lesson and he tells 'em to come back next evening and be treated. So back they go next night and he says "You got to go in the side room, one at a time, to be shaved and treated." So in they go, and who do you think is there, why the District Nurse . . . can't think of her name . . . but that great ol' gal with arms as thick as telephone poles. You didn't mess her about. "Right" she say, "down with 'em!" Blast man, they was terrified. She'd got this great ol' cut-throat. They thought as how they was gonna be gelded! When she'd finished with the razor she smacks on a poultice of iodine and carbolic. That wholly stung – I don't reckon them lads had a mite of sleep for a week. But o'course the trouble had only just started.'

'What trouble?' I ventured.

'Well, that itch was on the move. Others were getting it. That had already spread about the village.'

'How do you mean spread?'

'Well, the itch was caused by little old mites. Stands to reason they'd start jumping about, 'ticular when they see a lot of strappin' healthy people after they been use to livin' on them 'nemic London lot.'

'Hang on,' I protested, 'are you trying to tell me it was some sort of flea?'

'No, these is worse than an old flea 'cause you can't see 'em they're so small, but they jump just as far. An old flea's no trouble. If you get one of they on yer you can soon poke about and nip 'em out with finger and thumb. Anyways, within a couple of weeks half the folk in the village were scratchin' and the doctor had near run out of iodine and carbolic. I remember my old gal a comin' home from church one Sunday and sayin' the vicar had been scratchin' under his armpits all through his sermon. He was bound to get the itch; plenty of meat on him. 'Course, silly old beggar didn't do nothin' about it directly. Come the next Tuesday he goes to address the Mother's Union in the church hall and afore the meeting's over every old gal in the place is scratchin' away.'

Despite my scepticism I managed a laugh.

'No laughin' matter,' he scolded, 'when a woman's got to fry bacon and egg and scratch at the same time there could be a nasty accident.'

Old Newson stopped to pop a peppermint into his mouth. After a few sucks he continued.

'Weren't only the folks that was troubled, everywhere you went the cats and dogs had their paws agoin' like mad. And tha's the best time I ever remember for shootin' rabbits. They was so busy scratchin' they didn't bother to run.'

This was all getting a bit too far-fetched for me but old Newson was in full stride.

'Remember Rue Scrutts' brother Albert what had that small-holding up Chapel Hill Lane? Kept an old Shorthorn in his orchard and he noticed that keep rubbin' its rear end up against trees. Someone told him that it had the itch and he better do something about it. Well, he were too mean to ever call the vet, so he mixes up his own poultice of disinfectant, wasp poison and Harpic. Then the old fool puts a halter on the cow, ties it up to an apple tree, lifts its tail and slaps the poultice on. Man, that old Shorthorn nearly took off; that went round that tree so fast it nearly dunged in its own face. The halter broke and that was gone outa the gate and up the road like a bullet. Reckon that holds the world speed record for cows. Went miles afore old Albert could catch it. Didn't itch any more – didn't milk any more neither.'

'When did this epidemic die out?' I queried, hoping to bring comments on the topic to a close as it was difficult to concentrate on the starter motor.

'Never did stop completely; over these past 50 year there's been several that's been hit by it from time to time. Not as bad as it were in the Thirties I'll grant yer. Rue Scrutt's the last I can remember, he was itchin' something awful three or four years ago – same year as he got a long service medal at the Suffolk Show. 'Course, he never should have been allowed to go.'

'Why?' I knew he wanted me to ask.

'Well, he was bound to spread the itch weren't he. When I saw him shaking hands with the Duke of . . . what's his name? There's so many of them royal dukes now I can't remember their names. Anyways, when I saw them shaking hands I said to my missus, "You mark my word, that Duke'll be gettin' the itch!" And I reckon I was right too, 'cause only last week I see him on tele reviewin' some troops and all the time he's scratchin' the back of his neck.'

Old Newson raised himself up on his stick and made for the workshop door. 'Well, I can see how's your busy so I'll be off.' With that he departed, only to poke his grinning face round the door again a few seconds later. 'Prince Charles were scratchin' his nose a lot on tele last night. I'll be keepin' an eye on the Queen from now on.'

I didn't believe a word of it. All the same scratching isn't the pleasure it was.

Essex County Council

Many libraries in Essex have
facilities for exhibitions
and meetings —

enquire at your local library
for details